The Street

Also by Bernardine Bishop

Unexpected Lessons in Love
Hidden Knowledge

Praise for UNEXPECTED LESSONS IN LOVE

'This is one of the most enjoyable books I've read in years. I found it completely gripping. The carefully but unobtrusively structured plot (involving adoption, DNA and paternity) is domestic but with a wide reach; it is played out against a backdrop of world events. On reflection, I have never before read a book which confronts a serious and almost unmentionable illness with such lightness of touch. It's happy and it's cheering, with a beautiful warmth to it, achieved without a moment of sentimentality. I loved it.'   Margaret Drabble

'Bishop treats a fearful subject with an extraordinary lightness of touch; her humour and her emotional wisdom make this a delightful and humane novel.'   *The Times*

'Warm and emotionally convincing . . . effortlessly graceful'   *Sunday Times*

'Bishop is a fine, intelligent writer, capable of handling moral and philosophical themes with a light touch'   *Sunday Telegraph*

'It's impossible to recommend the late Bernardine Bishop's wondrous book too highly'   *Guardian*

'Full of humour, kindness and gentle irony, this is a richly satisfying read'   *Sunday Mirror*

'This novel, wise, sharp and startlingly frank, distils a lifetime of reflection on the rules of attraction, affection – and family life. From confused youth to the ordeals and confusions of old age, her wry insights delight.'   *Independent*

'A remarkable, immensely readable and warm-hearted book.'   *Sunday Express*

'This is a vibrant and ever welcoming novel . . . it offers such a rich range of pleasures.'
Observer

'A wonderful novel, one of those rare books which leaves the reader with a deeper understanding of the human heart . . . This is an author of exceptional intelligence, subtlety and warmth.'   *Spectator*

'A charming, playful novel.'   *Red*

'A refreshingly candid, unexpectedly witty and ultimately moving tale.'   *Candis*

'Considered and reflective, humorous and entertaining, this is a surprising and moving novel'
Good Book Guide

'Exquisite, funny and sad'   *Times Literary Supplement*

'This is the sort of story which grabs you, pulls you in and won't let you go – but in a very gentle way. The characters are superb. It's wise and it's witty. It's sublimely well-written, not with flowery literary devices but in the sort of prose that leaves you surprised when you realise that you've read a hundred pages and you've no intention of giving up just yet . . . I was left with a warm glow when I finished reading.'   *Bookbag*

The Street

BERNARDINE BISHOP

SCEPTRE

First published in Great Britain in 2015 by Sceptre
An imprint of Hodder & Stoughton
An Hachette UK company

1

A CIP catalogue record for this title is
available from the British Library

ISBN 978 1 444 78982 9
Ebook ISBN 978 1 444 78925 6

Typeset in Adobe Caslon Pro by Palimpsest Book Production Limited,
Falkirk, Stirlingshire

Printed and bound by Clays Ltd, St Ives plc

Hodder & Stoughton policy is to use papers that are natural, renewable and
recyclable products and made from wood grown in sustainable forests. The logging
and manufacturing processes are expected to conform to the environmental
regulations of the country of origin.

Hodder & Stoughton Ltd
338 Euston Road
London NW1 3BH

www.hodder.co.uk

Chapter 1

Sometimes it is impossible to turn even a short London street into a village. But sometimes it can be easily done. It all depends on one or two personalities.

Palmerston Street was a short street. It had twenty-eight front doors, fourteen even numbers on one side and fourteen odd numbers on the other. Each side was a row of Victorian cottages. Long since, they had all been built on to at the back, creating an extra room or two, to the shrinkage of the small gardens. Some had lofts added; others, less satisfactorily because of the proximity of an underground river, had cellars rendered habitable. Some had both.

Palmerston Street was less of a village than some residents would have liked it to be, but more so than suited others. The majority of the households will not come into this story. The people who lived in the houses that will not figure had been urban for generations, did not think in terms of neighbours and neighbourhoods, but got on with busy lives in other places and circles, or in houses that changed hands often, and never settled down in long owner-ship. Most households noticed and had an attitude to the village spirit in the street, either welcoming it, feeling intrigued and embraced, or hating the notion that strangers might know their business and that there might be the twitch of a lace curtain. Such divisions could exist even within a household.

Anne Darwin was a retired property surveyor in her late sixties. Those of the street who took note of the street's atmosphere thought Anne was at the centre of what made the street a community. Community was Anne's word; some people liked it, others did not. Anne had a history of making communities out of collections of people, be they streets, offices, or parents at the schools her daughter attended. To some she was a treasure, to others, a pain.

In good weather she would often stand outside her house for half an hour in the afternoon, her dark cardigan stretched double by crossed arms, her thin figure full of expectation, her eyes darting up and down the street. Lonely people, gossipy people, people with little children, people who were her friends, would stop and talk to her. She was the grapevine. If a house in the street was for sale, she was the person to come to for the low-down. Some conversations were fleeting, others long. Sometimes several neighbours simultaneously would stop in their tracks and collect around her.

Her husband, Eric, did not share her interest, nor approve of her enthusiasm. When she stood at their gate, he would sometimes look out of the front window at her eager, lithe back view. He hid behind the curtain and peered, in case she looked round, and in case his curiosity was spotted by one of her prey. As far as he knew, he was struggling with uncomfortable emotions of contempt and embarrassment. But he also felt the pain of exclusion. Anne was surviving retirement, in a way he was not able to. She had found a new interest. It was a pathetic interest, but Eric had not found an interest at all.

When he learned that he and Anne were to have a grandson staying with them, he had a sinking feeling that Anne hoped this would be an interest for him, and that it would not be. Their daughter and husband had to be in Canada for a year, and had decided to leave John in London with his grandparents to start the good secondary school in which they had secured him a place. The two younger children were to go to Canada with their parents. So there were two new things in Eric's life: retirement; and the approaching advent of John, aged eleven.

The four adults involved had not seriously wondered whether John would be all right. His parents were stimulated and preoccupied by the prospect of their year abroad. John would come to Canada and join them for the Christmas holiday. They put it to John that September to December is not very long. It was exciting for John, they told each other, to be starting big school, and lucky that the school was walking distance from Palmerston Street. Everything, from their point of view, was falling into place.

On her part, Anne's mind had turned immediately to rooms and spaces within her house. John could have the attic, which surely a child would like. Anne liked a challenge, and was prepared to throw herself into this one; but it occurred to her to wish that she knew John better. The young family had lived in Edinburgh and Manchester so far, which hadn't favoured easy meetings with the children's maternal ancestry. Anne had been known to wonder, disloyally, why John was not to be boarded with his other grandparents; they lived in Edinburgh, so John must at least at one time have seen more of then. But it was to be London for Clifford and Sara after Toronto, so they were establishing John in London, which made perfect sense.

Eric alone gave way to a qualm, and said to Anne, 'Won't John miss his family?' To which Anne, who thought Eric was trying to get out of it, answered breezily, 'We *are* his family.'

It was still August, so there was a fortnight's grace before John's arrival. Late August in the street saw inhabitants returning from holidays. There was unpacking of cars, there were shouted greetings and welcoming waves. Window-boxes had been faithfully watered, cats fed, and those who had discharged these obligations breathed small sighs of relief. Anne stood at her front gate; Eric watched unwillingly from inside the house.

Eric was a hoarder, or so Anne thought. One of the effects of this characteristic was that he still had his boyhood books. In this fortnight he took to climbing to and from the attic, furnishing what were to be John's quarters with appropriate classics. Anne liked to hear his heavy tread up and down the ladder, proving that he was taking an interest and, in his own way, providing for John. Sometimes she stopped whatever she was doing and listened, just to hear him.

'It's a bit hot up there,' Eric said to Anne. He was a big man, and his broad forehead was sweating.

'Have you opened the skylights?'

'No. I thought pigeons might come in.'

'Pigeons?'

'There's pigeon shit on the glass.'

Taken aback, Anne considered. Eventually she said, 'When the room's inhabited, they won't want to come in.'

Eric didn't answer, and was having a drink of water. 'Hot work,' he said.

Later, Anne went up to the attic, her feet brisker and less creaky on the narrow steps than Eric's. She wished she knew whether John was the kind of person who had to pee in the night. She did not like the idea of his coming up and down the ladder half asleep. She had put an elegant red plastic bucket in a corner of the attic, but she knew it would be difficult for her to put into words to John what it was potentially for.

4

A mild thrill of excitement ran through her whenever she saw the attic. It was the kind of excitement that goes straight back to childhood. The attic was so big, so quiet, so bare, and so neat. It had its own smell – slightly musty and out-housy, but pleasant. An adult could stand at full height only in the middle; it would be easier for John. There were two skylights, and when, as now, it was sunny, they threw geometrical shapes of yellow on to the floor. There was a chest of drawers, a desk, a chair for the desk, a radiator, and a book case. There was a futon, on which Anne had arranged pretty, patterned bedding. With its minimal furniture, well spread out, the attic appeared sparse, almost monastic, but it was spacious, spanning the length and breadth of the house. Eric had said if they were doing anything up there they might as well have a full loft conversion, and make a proper room of it, or two, improving the value of the house. Anne had wanted a much less ambitious job, keeping the contours of the roof and putting in little more than insulation, a floor and a ceiling. Then there had been the skylights and the electricity. Finally the blue fitted carpet, which made the space look even bigger. People did not often sleep up here, as the Darwins had a spare bedroom. But Anne loved the idea that the attic was there, and now she was pleased that it would come into its own for John.

Bending her head when necessary, and finally walking with a crouch, Anne studied the books Eric had been putting in the shelves. Stevenson – *Treasure Island*, *The Black Arrow*, *Kidnapped*, and some poems. A long row of faded, hardback Hornblowers. Five or six Swallows and Amazons. *King Solomon's Mines*. The Jungle Books. Several Biggles. Anne was touched by Eric's choices. She knew she might have been confronted by the spines of *Ivanhoe* and *Beowulf*, favourites which happily seemed to have been rejected, and must still be reposing on Eric's own shelves. She could, if Eric's judgement had failed him completely, have been offended by the title of *Lorna Doone*. Or *Kim*.

Now she looked at the desk, scribbled-on, wooden and steady, Sara's desk actually. Perhaps she could tell John that. The surface was big enough for a laptop, without the laptop having to take up all the space, and there were four drawers, which Anne now checked were empty. Immediately above the desk was the trap door to the roof, renewed by the builders, and tidily bolted. Beside that was a smoke alarm. All seemed in order.

Anne opened one of the skylights. Her head popped out into warm, bright air. The white clouds seemed very near. It was odd, and nice, not to be able to see downwards, but only upwards. There could be no checking whether a neighbour was going by. She could hear pigeons, but could not see them, and the purring noise was soothing. She decided to leave the skylight open for the moment, but would have to remember to come up to close it if there was a threat of rain.

Because she was so high and so sequestered, she did not hear the doorbell, and by the time she was downstairs, Eric had gone to the door, and was in conversation with Georgia Fox. Georgia saw Anne appear behind Eric, and called, 'Oh, Anne.'

Anne pushed forward. 'Has something happened?'

'Brenda has been taken to hospital. Didn't you see the ambulance?'

'No. What's happened?'

'I don't know. It was all incredibly quick. Five minutes ago. I heard the ambulance, it stopped outside Brenda's, I was still wondering what was happening and whether to go over, when a stretcher came out, then off they went. Didn't you hear the ambulance?'

'No. Come in, Georgia.'

It was worrying for both of them not to understand something that happened in the street, and Anne made tea. Eric withdrew, not as incurious as he hoped to seem. Anne and Georgia sat in Anne's kitchen, each with a frown of concern on her face.

'Has she seemed unwell?' Anne asked.

'Not really,' said Georgia, hoping she had not been negligent. 'I went in yesterday morning, and we did the crossword. Brenda was still in bed, but she always is, until her carers come. Oh dear, I wish I had gone in this morning.' She paused. 'I'd better go in now. No one will have fed the cat.'

'I'll come with you.'

Together they hurried up the street. Anne was energised by a crisis which did not affect her emotions; she did not know Brenda well. Georgia loved Brenda, and was puzzled about how to get news of her. It was not known, even, which hospital she had been taken to.

When Georgia, who had the key, let them in to Brenda's house, two carers, known to Georgia, in bright blue uniforms, were sitting in the kitchen, making notes and phone calls.

'It must be you who called the ambulance,' said Georgia. 'Which hospital has she gone to?'

The carers confirmed this deduction, and gave the name of the hospital. 'We've fed Ben,' said one of them, seeing Georgia look round for the cat. In fact Benn had two n's to his name, for he was called after Tony Benn. He would have been called Tony, but for Tony Blair.

The story came out. The carers had arrived and let themselves in as usual. They had called out as usual, but, unusually, there was no answering cry. The senior carer's fingers had been on her mobile almost as they entered Brenda's bedroom. 'I thought she had passed away.'

'And had she?'

'We thought so, and so did the paramedics, but they took her, anyway, because that's routine. If there's a chance.'

'We'll miss her,' said the smaller carer, who had not spoken yet.

'She wouldn't want to be resuscitated,' said Georgia, quietly crying.

Brenda Byfleet, who had lived in the street for decades, going from the briskness of early middle age to a housebound ninety, was not famous. But Georgia Fox had heard of her, and been thrilled to discover, ten years ago, that Brenda lived in a house near the one she was buying. Georgia was over a generation younger than Brenda. When Georgia became involved in peace projects, Brenda Byfleet was a big name, in that small world. Brenda had not missed a step of any of the Aldermaston marches. She had lived for three years on Greenham Common. She had chained herself to railings. She had been in prison. She had distributed leaflets and organised petitions. In old age she had marched, or limped, against the attacks on Afghanistan and Iraq. On the terrible evening when she realised that this last, enormous march had cut no ice with the government, she sat and cried. 'We have achieved nothing,' she said to Georgia.

In a curious way, inconspicuous to both, by the time of Brenda's death, each of these two women had become the most important person in the other's life. It should be said that people were not very important to either, in an intimate sense; so the competition was not severe. Brenda's lifelong singleness arose, at least in part, from her singleness of purpose. She had family money from tea plantations, which income source worried her terribly; but, on the other hand, it was convenient not to have to earn. She balanced the good she hoped she did against the exploitative nature of her daily bread.

For unmarried women in Brenda's generation, to be a virgin was not seriously eccentric. No one marvelled at it in Brenda's case, for she was neither beautiful nor charming, and had never thought to try to be. She was direct, loud-voiced, opinionated and well-informed. She was energetic and stout, with unkempt hair, and she never gave clothes a thought, unless she had to speak publicly or go to a do or a funeral, which occasions made her stare helplessly at her clothes until friends assembled a uniform for her. Women and men were her friends indiscriminately, and if there were no common causes, the friendships failed unnoticed. Her warmth and her laugh attracted people to her, her command of current facts, and her courage.

And now she was dead. Georgia had phoned the hospital, and heard the news. She put down the receiver and stared out of the window. Brenda's house looked the same as always, and poor Benn was sitting on the doorstep, washing a paw. Georgia's own doorbell rang. It was Anne.

'You must be upset,' she said to Georgia.

'I can't believe it,' Georgia said. 'That's the main feeling.'

Together they looked at Brenda's house. Finally Georgia said, 'What about the cat?'

'I'll have him,' said Anne, who always liked stepping in. She hoped she would not regret it. Might a cat be an interest for Eric? And nice for John?

Nieces, never seen before, came to Brenda's house. It was Anne who found out that they were nieces, and that when they had cleared the house, they planned to sell it. Georgia and Anne went to Brenda's cremation, organised by the nieces, quick and disappointing. On the evening of the cremation, Georgia took a key, and rather furtively, crossed the road to Brenda's house. She wanted to say some sort of goodbye. It was Brenda's small and untidy study that she particularly wanted to see, and be in, for the last time. It had a cluttered desk, no curtains, and photos pinned to the walls. There was a special smell, and there was the battered armchair in which Georgia had been sitting when Brenda said, 'We have achieved nothing,' and cried, with those terrible hoarse sobs. Georgia was nervous, for her visit was illicit, and her existence not known to the nieces. She turned the key in the lock as so often before, but the door resisted utterly. She pushed. Then she realised the nieces had deadlocked the door, as well they might. Georgia's latchkey made it do no more than shift a millimetre. Brenda never used the deadlock, and Georgia had not imagined there was one, nor noticed its disused keyhole. Such a thing was inimical to Brenda. Georgia hurried home. The house was alien territory now, and Georgia relinquished any claim to it.

Georgia and Anne had not been real friends until now. They were both people who liked the street to be a street, or, as some would say, the street to be a soap; and that had always been a link. But they were no more than warm acquaintances. Anne did not even know what Georgia did for a living. But Brenda's death brought them together. Together they walked down the street rattling a box of cat biscuits, calling and mewing, to lure Benn to his new home. This project involved a number of expeditions, for Benn would eat the offered biscuit in Anne's kitchen, then jump out of the window to make his way back to Brenda's locked front door. Other neighbours took food to him there, which did not help. Anne and Georgia found licked plates on Brenda's doorstep. Then Anne managed to put it about that she was taking Benn, and the project of Benn's house-move became a street project. Meanwhile Eric was working on a cat-flap in the Darwins' back door.

'I don't even know what you do,' said Anne to Georgia,

when they had despairingly watched Benn's muscular tabby hindquarters disappear out of the window yet again. 'Is he ever going to feel at home here?'

'Give him time,' said Georgia. 'Well, I'm a zoologist.'

'Zoologist? What sort? Academic?'

'Yes.' Georgia mentioned where she worked.

'Well.' Anne was strangely pleased.

'Gastropods,' said Georgia, encouraged by the expression on Anne's face. 'Molluscs. Snails, really.'

'Snails!' said Anne, only ever having thought of them as a garden pest. 'Snails. Eric wages war on them in the garden.'

'I wish he wouldn't. And everyone does. The garden snail is fast becoming an endangered species.'

~

After three or four more days Benn felt able to sit and wash on a chair in Anne's kitchen, rather than making a dash for it the minute he had eaten. Eric and Anne both felt proud to see him there. He had accepted them. The next day he worked Eric's cat-flap, and Eric felt honoured. Georgia wondered what had happened in Benn's mind to enable him to make the transition. She did not like to think it had been easy.

'I suppose Brenda will be forgotten,' she said sadly to Eric and Anne.

'Won't she have an obituary?' said Anne.

'She hasn't had one in the *Independent*,' said Eric.

'Nor in the *Guardian*,' said Georgia.

They were silent.

'She didn't have any children, that's the problem,' said Anne, then could have bitten her tongue, for Georgia didn't either.

But luckily Georgia didn't seem to be listening. After half

a minute she looked up, and said, 'So when it comes down to it, what is a life?'

'What do you mean, what is a life?' said Eric. 'Here we are, we are born, we live, we die, some of us after shorter lives, some longer.'

'But all Brenda's thoughts, passions, letters to prime ministers, letters to . . . All her direct action, conversations, hopes, memories, yes, memories! going back to the peace movement before the war, the thirties – all that, leave alone her personal life . . . All gone.'

'She should have written a book,' said Anne. Georgia felt that people always say this, as a way of avoiding the question, what is a life?

When Georgia got home, happy and not happy that there was no Benn sitting patiently on Brenda's doorstep, she started wondering whether to put together an 'Other Lives' on Brenda for the *Guardian*. She was baulked by the lack of solid information. She had only known Brenda for the last decade of Brenda's nine, and they had no mutual friends. The impulse faded.

But the impact of Brenda's death did not fade. Georgia had just started a sabbatical year, her last, as within the next seven years she would retire. She had been looking forward to her sabbatical, and thought she was full of research interests. In November she was going to join a project studying the special qualities of the shells of desert snails in the Sinai. It had been very exciting to be invited on this prestigious enterprise. She had intended to do a lot of work beforehand, starting now. But because of Brenda, the heart had gone out of it.

It was not only that she missed Brenda, nor only that a close death brings all death closer. She was also struggling with a sense of the vanity of human endeavour. Seventy years, at a guess, of aspiration, resilience, toil and dedication; and what was there to show for Brenda? What was there to show for what she had striven for? And yet, what else is there to do in a life, but try to make things better? Or, in Georgia's own case, to add a tiny bit to what we know about snails?

Chapter 2

On the designated day, a fine sunny one in early September, Clifford, Sara, John, and the two little ones erupted at Anne and Eric's. Their luggage filled the front passage of the house, trunk on trunk, but it was not going to stay there, for all but John were taking a flight to Toronto that evening. The house was crowded and noisy. Benn fled upstairs to Eric and Anne's bedroom. Anne was trying to provide a big tea. Eric decided to take the children into the garden, to lessen the concentration of noise. That suited Fabia, seven, and Tom, five; but John stayed with the grown-ups.

Clifford and Sara were full of plans, and of the excitement of travel, Clifford booming, Sara declaiming. Clifford talked to no one in particular; Sara to her mother. Then Clifford went into the garden, and boomed to Eric. Besides trying to listen to plans and be the right sort of mother, Anne had two feelings. One was longing for the time when they would leave. The other was sudden uncertainty about how she would cope with John when they did. Neither of these feelings could be communicated to Sara. This did not matter, for Sara did all the talking.

Anne had had a picture of the family sitting round the kitchen table for tea. She had laid the table with this in view. She was making a big pot of tea, and there was juice. But soon Eric came in and collected the plate of buttered buns and took them outside. 'I want a drink,' whispered Fabia, suddenly appearing and clinging shyly to her mother's arm, and the juice went outside as well. Anne poured tea for herself and Sara. John did not want anything. He was sitting on the floor in the corner of the room playing a game on his mobile phone.

Clifford came in for the cake, made by Anne, who had visualised a more ceremonious cutting of it; and that was the end of the civilised tea. Sara told Anne about the house in Toronto, the anticipated difficulties on the flight with the children, the excellences of the school they had found for John, and asked if his uniform had arrived, which it had not.

'It will tomorrow, then. And the school's so near you!' she said. 'That's so wonderful. You or Dad will walk him the first day, then he'll know the way himself. Won't you, darling? He's good at all that. We can talk on the phone and we can skype, it'll hardly be like being separated at all.'

Anne wanted to ask Sara if John peed at night, but couldn't with John in the room. She suggested going to view John's room. The attic had not been converted until after Sara had left home, so it was new to her as well. The three of them trooped upstairs, carrying John's cases, Anne leading, then Sara, then John, and they continued up the ladder in that formation. Each emerged in turn into the large and quiet space. Sara was delighted, and told John how much he would love it. There was not much to do up there, and time was getting on, so they came down again. They found Eric, Clifford and the children in the kitchen; the men were trying to wash the children's sticky hands at the sink. Tom was whimpering because his fingers had been mildly scalded, a point contested by his father. Soon Eric, intensely relieved that this moment had arrived, was ringing for a taxi, and the children were being sorted out for departure. There was a crisis about Fabia's wool dog, which she would need on the aeroplane. Suddenly they were going, and the taxi driver was helping with the cases. But where was John? Anne hurried upstairs, calling, and he emerged from the attic.

'Time to say goodbye,' said Anne. Her voice was cheerful, but she tried to put a bit of sympathy in it as well, just in case.

Fabia and Tom were already in the taxi, so John did not have to say goodbye to them. His father gave him a quick hug and a 'See you at Christmas, be good.' Then Sara put her arms round John, brief and breezy, and he gripped her with all his strength, his face pressed against her coat. After a full minute she gave a little laugh, and looked round the watching faces. That was the moment to extricate herself, but she could not. John knew his mother, and knew exactly how long any hug was likely to last, and the intended brevity of this one made him cling on even tighter. He was using her coat to stop his face from breaking up, but he knew it was not working. How could it work, when his nose was buried in her smell? In absolute silence, he clung to her, knowing he was making a fool of himself, and fearing it, but refusing to let go.

'Don't make me cry, darling,' said Sara.

In the end, Clifford gave him a pull, gentle but no-nonsense, and said, 'You don't want Granny and Grandpa to think you're a baby!' Sara twitched the handful of coat away from his clutch, and the taxi was gone. John groped blindly for the front door, and ran upstairs.

Neither grandparent had expected this. When Eric saw John hanging on to his mother, he choked, almost audibly, his boarding school agonies brought back to him. Anne had endured a qualm when John entered the house that he would be stony-faced and difficult to get to know, but she had not thought of him as floridly upset. Not willing to blame him, she blamed Sara. Eric's and Anne's eyes met, both faces obviously disconcerted, even appalled. Anne noticed Eric's watery look, and was annoyed, fearing she would be offered sentimentality rather than help. They stood silently. Both were feeling failures.

'I'd better get things in from the garden,' said Eric. Troubled, he collected the remains of the buns and the ruins of the cake, and various cups and juice cartons. When he came indoors Anne was standing just where he had left her, wondering what a proper grandmother would do. Would such a person run upstairs after John, longing to hug and console? That prospect embarrassed her, for what if she were rejected? Should she wait for him to come downstairs, and should she have hot buttered scones at the ready? Or would that be denial? She sighed. It was coming home to her that, if she loved John, she would know what to do. Everyone including herself had assumed she loved him, but she did not, or not yet. That was why it was difficult to know what a proper grandmother would do.

Eric was washing up. Anne went over to him, and looked up into his face. 'What shall I do?'

'Better leave him. He'll have to come down in the end. He'll get hungry!' Eric said this, even managing a little jollity, but actually he had no idea what to do. There are pangs that make hunger impossible, and he knew it. He was glad that it was more Anne's problem than his.

'Sara should have warned us,' said Anne.

'What difference would that have made?' said Eric, rinsing.

'She must have known,' said Anne.

Things about her daughter that she had never liked came into Anne's mind – a flightiness, supposed to be charming and disarming, about responsibility; its always being up to Anne to remember the dancing shoes on Wednesdays, even when Sara was quite big; Sara's insistence on a hamster, which Anne and Eric soon had to look after; the guitar lessons of which Sara tired as soon as she found she wasn't a genius. Anne did not want to be feeling like this towards her daughter, particularly when Sara was so soon to be in an aeroplane which might crash. She decided to make the scones anyway, and perhaps the smell of them, drifting upstairs, would cheer John and bring him down in his own time. Then they could all three have a conversation as if nothing had happened. And scones would go some way to making her feel a proper grandmother.

But nothing was going to cheer John for the moment. He lay on the futon with his face in the pillow, letting the tears out at last, writhing stiffly, gasping. The fact that he could not bear this did not mean he did not have to. He knew that. Every thought made it worse – the thought that Fab and Tom were with Mummy and Daddy and he was not; the thought that Mum imagined he was happy, or soon would be, for he knew her well enough to be sure of that; the thought that he would have somehow to hide all that he felt from Granny and Grandpa. He ground his face into the bed, and kicked a little. This half-hour would be present to John all his life.

He rolled over, looked up and saw the skylights. They lifted his heart a little. They seemed to represent a way out – a way out of this frightening house and away from these unknown people. He got up, and went over to the sunnier of the two. He saw how the windows worked, and, climbing on to his desk, tilted one open. His head popped out. He could see tiles, houses opposite, sky. He was quite alone. He stood there. It occurred to him that the sky was the same in Canada as it was in England. It was the same sky. Then he turned his head the other way and saw a pigeon. It was standing on the tiles quite close to him. Then another pigeon joined it.

In the rest of his life, he would never be the same as he had been until today, because this pain, at the age of eleven, when he was still somewhat molten, was too bad. But by the same token he became for the rest of his life a person who could search out consolations. The sky, and the fact that Canada was under the same sky, was a consolation. The pigeons were another. The pigeons were a consolation because they were free. They held the slanting tiles safely with their pink claws. They jerked and cooed. Then they flew away, together. But they had been there, the feathers of their necks glinting green and purple. He felt he had friends of whom the people downstairs knew nothing. He could have a world that was not their world, and he could survive.

There was a sandwich somewhere in his packing, that Mum had given him and he had not been able to eat. He cried afresh to see it, because Mum had made it. He pressed it briefly to his cheek. Then he broke it in half and put his head out of the window again. He laid both halves of the sandwich on the tiles, and waited. The pigeons did not come.

In spite of that, he now had enough energy to unpack his cases. He squashed his clothes into the chest of drawers. He put his laptop on the desk, and found a socket where he could plug it in. His laptop represented freedom, and privacy as well, for on that he could skype with Mum. Perhaps. Though Mum was not much good with the computer. By the time he had finished sorting out his things, he could hear a noise on his roof. He looked out. The pigeons had come back, and were pecking vigorously at his sandwich. They might be different pigeons from the first two. He could not tell. Their necks shone green and purple like the first ones. Two more fluttered along, seeing that something was up, and John watched them with intense satisfaction.

Eric was deputed to go up and bring John down. John heard his feet approaching. Then Eric's shaggy head appeared at the trap-door.

'Hullo ullo ullo,' said Eric. 'Aren't you coming down? It's nearly supper-time.'

John was at the computer. 'Hullo, Grandpa,' he said politely. Then, 'Can you give me the WiFi password?'

More of Eric emerged. 'Shall I put it in for you? If I can remember it.'

John slipped off the chair and Eric sat down with a creak. John could see a bald patch in the middle of Eric's head. The bald patch had wrinkles in it, like frowns. John wondered if Eric knew about the bald patch and the wrinkles. He would not be able to see them himself. Then it came home to him that Grandpa was Mum's father. Better not think that, in case the mention of Mum in his mind made him cry.

'This was your mother's desk,' said Eric, putting in the password. 'When she was a schoolgirl.'

John was silent, managing his face and his throat. He swallowed.

Eric finished and stood up. 'Now, down we go,' he said. 'I'll be taking you to school tomorrow. Do you have a uniform, or anything like that?'

'The uniform hasn't arrived,' John said. 'I think Granny knows about it.' John had forgotten this worry amongst the worse ones, and now his heart sank at the thought of being the only one in ordinary clothes tomorrow.

The scones were cold, but very nice to nibble with jam when they were produced after the shepherd's pie and peas. John managed a good meal, having eaten nothing all day, and Anne was relieved.

'John says his uniform hasn't arrived,' said Eric to Anne. 'Why hasn't it, if it was supposed to?'

John liked to hear this. You could never tell if grown-ups had taken things on board. He wouldn't have known how to raise the matter himself. He was warming to Grandpa.

'Just one of Sara's muddles,' said Anne. 'But it will definitely arrive tomorrow, so John will only have to go one day in mufti.'

'What's mufti?' asked John, alarmed. Suppose it was like woad.

'Ordinary clothes,' said Eric. 'What you're wearing now.'

'But my teeshirt is dirty,' said John.

'We'll find a clean one,' said Anne, smiling encouragingly at him. 'You will look fine. Anyway, first day of big school, probably other children won't have uniforms either.'

That was consoling. But the phrase 'first day of big school' reawakened secret misgivings.

'A boy in the street, Heironimo Pace, is in the second year at your school. Perhaps you will make friends with him. Number Eighteen.' This was Anne.

'And a girl,' said Eric to Anne, questioningly.

'No, Tallulah is still at primary school,' said Anne. 'It's her last year. But you will get to know them both. They are the only children your sort of age in the street.'

John was thinking at least he didn't have a long name, even if he would have no uniform, and did not live in an ordinary home.

'We must introduce John to Benn,' said Eric.

'Where is he?' asked Anne.

'He's still upstairs on our bed.'

'He's a cat,' said Anne to John.

'Can I see him?' said John. And seeing and stroking the big tabby cat, who indeed was stretched out on the double bed, purring, and reaching a lazy, friendly paw in John's direction, was soothing for John, like the pigeons.

But John hated the alien bathroom, with its unfamiliar smell, and quaked at the touch of the nice warm towel Anne put out for him, so unlike the thin damp ones used communally by his family. He refused a bath, not wanting to take off a stitch of clothes until he was on his own in his attic. He cringed when Anne tried to tell him about the bucket in the attic and its use. In this new life, no bodily intimacy must be conceded. He said goodnight and went upstairs. Granny was going to call him at seven. He cried into his pillow. Then he heard a slight noise, and got out of bed. Was it the pigeons? He poked his head out to see, but they were not there. The noise came again, and he realised it was from inside the house. He looked through the trap-door to the floor below. Benn was sharpening his claws on the carpet at the foot of the ladder. John lay flat on the floor and stretched a hand down.

'Come up,' he said.

Benn looked up and miaowed an answer, but did not want to try the ladder.

'Come on,' said John. 'You can do it.'

But apparently Benn couldn't, and John went back to bed.

~

'Shall we drop in on the Paces,' said Anne, 'and tell them John has arrived?'

'We can't both,' said Eric, washing up, his back to the room.

Silence from Anne, as she took in Eric's meaning. 'I'd clean forgotten about babysitting,' she said. 'My goodness.'

'We've probably forgotten a lot,' said Eric. 'But it'll come back.'

'We're out to dinner twice next week,' said Anne. 'I never thought.' She sat down, the better to digest a fuller understanding of the differences John was going to make to their life.

'You go up to the Paces if you like,' said Eric.

So Anne went up to the Paces, wondering whom she might ask to babysit, or sit, rather, as John was eleven, for the two nights in the coming week. There were quite a lot of people in the street she could approach, including Georgia, who lived next door to the Paces. John would not know anyone, though, and as it was John's first week, perhaps the two social events should be cancelled. She suspected that Eric would think this the best answer; but he never looked forward to dinners out anyway. If she was going to cancel, the sooner the politer. How strange of her, thought Anne, walking up the street in the warm September dusk, to have forgotten that sitters were now going to be a necessity of life.

She arrived at the Paces' house, with its battered fence, broken gate, and dead window-box, and was about to ring the bell. Her hand froze. She heard loud voices. She stood and listened. It was the Paces having one of their legendary rows. She had heard about the Paces' rows from various people who lived at their end of the street. Not from Georgia, because it was not the sort of thing Georgia talked about. Anne herself had never overheard one before. It was much more horrible than she had imagined from the hearsay. The male and female voices were shouting at the same time, shouting over each other. Anne could not hear words, but the intensity of the conflict made her turn and steal away. She hesitated, then rang Georgia's bell. Georgia came to the door. The quarrel could be heard from next door, and Anne gestured with her thumb and made a shocked, questioning expression.

'Yes,' said Georgia. She looked slightly embarrassed in the face of Anne, almost as if she herself had been found out, or were at fault. 'Yes. It's all right. Don't worry. Harry and Tally are here. We're playing Scrabble.'

Anne thought of asking Georgia to tell Harry and Tally about John, but decided it wasn't the moment. She smiled at Georgia and threw her eyes heavenwards, then began to walk home, quickly traversing the barrage of sound into the calm of her own end of the street.

Chapter 3

Most of the women in the street, and it was the women, by and large, who took an interest in the matter, sympathised with Beale Pace. Sally Pace was very nice, indeed nicer than Beale. But there was a feeling that she would be difficult to be married to. She was ten years older than Beale, which made her forty-six to his thirty-six. Beale's gangling and coltish good looks contrasted with Sally's designer elegance and pretty blonde hair. The women in the street admired the way Sally turned herself out, and esteemed her high-powered job; but when Beale came out of the house with his unbrushed curls, jeans and a battered sheepskin jacket, their hearts melted, and they construed the core of last night's rumpus as recrimination against Beale for earning no money, rather than, for example, agonising doubts from Sally about Beale's fidelity.

The next morning Eric and John were walking up the street towards John's school.

'Make a note of the way,' said Eric.

'But what about coming back?' said John.

'Granny or I will meet you after school today.'

'And then I can make a note of the way back.'

'Yes. And then tomorrow if you're not sure . . .'

'I will be sure.'

'If you are, you are.'

Just then Harry was to be seen, coming out of the Paces' house. 'That chap goes to the same school as you, I think,' said Eric. John said nothing, afraid that Eric was going to try to catch up and introduce him. But Eric only said, 'You may get to know him, and his sister.' Now that the immediate danger of being introduced was over, John was able to inspect at a distance a back view of the school uniform. That boy was so lucky, wearing the uniform; too lucky even to know he was lucky. As the school drew closer, more and more examples of the uniform appeared, in all shapes and sizes, tailored to both genders, but always the same uniform.

'Will I have my uniform for tomorrow?' he asked Eric.

'Yes. Granny's going to make sure of that. She says she'll go to the shop herself if they can't deliver it today.'

John said no more, for fear of hearing his mum blamed. He was holding on to himself as it was.

~

In the Paces' house, Beale was still in bed, and Sally and Tally were having breakfast.

'But what were you quarrelling *about?*' Tally was asking in an undertone.

'Oh darling, you know Daddy. He always makes a mountain out of a molehill.'

'But will it still be a mountain this morning?'

'We will all be gone by the time he gets up, so we won't know.' Sally giggled conspiratorially, but met no response. So she said, 'First day of your last year in primary school.' Tally had nothing to offer to this. There was a look of anxiety in her eyes that would show all her life.

Sally tried again. 'There are rumours about a newcomer in the street. Anne Darwin's grandson. He'll be starting at Jibbs.'

'Do you think you are going to split up?'

Sally was silent. She had not anticipated this question.

'You see,' said Tally, testing how far she could tilt her glass of milk without it spilling over the edge, 'sometimes it sounds as if you hate each other.'

Sally was a bit annoyed by Tally's invitation into deep waters. She was in no doubt that Tally's worries mattered; but to think about them was a boring chore and irritating at this time of day. She smiled the dazzling smile both her children loved. She saw from Tally's face that she was bewitched but not reassured.

'We'll sort it out,' she said in the end. 'Don't worry. We don't hate each other. Jump in the car, darling.' So off they went, Tally to school, Sally to her office.

⁓

Beale woke up. He listened. He liked to hear noises from the kitchen as he scrambled into consciousness in the mornings, but usually, as today, he was too late. So he lay in the silence, and quite soon suffering came in.

To circumvent it, he struggled out of bed and headed for the kitchen. He put his hands on the sides of the cafetière to see if it was still hot, and then poured himself a cup of coffee and put it in the microwave. He rinsed the cafetière, and put the kettle on to make himself a new brew. At the same time he began washing up his family's breakfast: Harry's Shreddies, Tally's unfinished Frosties, Sally's toast and marmalade, various cups and glasses. The kettle came to the boil. He drank the left-over cup of coffee while the fresh brew waited. The room was filling with the comforting smell of coffee. He wiped the kitchen table, then swept the floor. For all these activities he was naked; watching the Paces' front window at this time of day tended to be a source of pleasant or shocked fascination for the neighbours opposite. It had been a pleasant one for

Brenda in her study, toiling over her Amnesty letters or writing to the Prime Minister; otherwise she would have died without ever seeing a naked man. Children late for school were often unjustly rewarded.

Beale showered and dressed. He put on a suit, which was unusual. Then he sat down to study his lines. He had an appointment for an audition, but only for a voice-over.

'It's not only a matter of where you live,' he read, mouthing the words mockingly, wagging his head. 'It is not only a matter of who you live with.' Shouldn't that be 'whom'? 'It is not only a matter of who you have been in the past, nor of who you may be in the future.' What on earth was it going to turn out to be a matter of, then? He sighed. What was this nonsense all about? He had forgotten. Cat food? Loo paper? The Tory party? He flipped the page. Insurance. Of course. He started again, speaking aloud now, and making his voice mysterious. 'It is not only a matter . . .'

Utterly demeaning, of course, but if he did not get this job he would earn no money this month.

He was distracted by not being able to make up his mind about whether he and Sally had made love the night before. He remembered the quarrel, but the quarrel, as usual, had started them drinking, and the latter part of the evening was difficult to recall. He threw aside 'It's not only a matter . . .' and headed for the bedroom. He was looking for evidence that she had shared the bed with him, but there was nothing conclusive. He passed into the spare room. Was there a clue that Sally had spent the night here? The duvet was straight, the window open. That proved nothing, for Sally would have tidied up as soon as she woke. It hurt him that he could not remember. He hated the callous person it implied. More important, if they had made love, he needn't worry about whether things would come right today. Things would have come right already. He would have regained his position as a person who could give Sally something, indeed could give her a pearl of great price. He secretly felt that he would have regained his position as lord and master, but this was no way to phrase it, not even in his mind.

They had been together thirteen years, and all that time Beale's self-esteem had depended entirely on the belief that Sally loved him. Was it love, exactly? Was it perhaps admiration? Was it that he could not live without feeling glamorous to Sally? Did he need to be adored? He was not sure. He was thinking this over now, back in the kitchen. Perhaps it was not something as grown-up as love that he needed. And the expression 'self-esteem' was wrong, as well. It was a term his therapist had imported to meet the case, but it was much too mild and mincing. It was more that Beale could not live, breathe, eat, think, sleep, if he felt that Sally was indifferent to him. He became like an animal with a mortal wound, dragging itself about. He would snarl and worry her until she resumed production of the elixir he needed. Then life could begin again.

None of this was great, he thought, but he and Sally had stayed together longer than a lot of their friends. All relationships have infantile elements. His therapist had been vehement about that. Of late Beale had stopped going to therapy, because it was expensive, and he did not want to keep it up on Sally's money, less from a sense of justice than because she might hold it against him. He did not miss his therapist. He went swimming instead, which was free.

He had not told Sally about the audition, because such an audition was contemptible. If he got the job, the money would slide silently into their shared bank account, as had the much larger sums he had earned in days gone by. It was years since his income had been comparable to Sally's. This imbalance made it more difficult to feel adored, or even manly. Beale was suffering. To make matters worse, he had quite a bad hangover.

~

'Would you like a cup of tea?' called Sally out of her window. She had come home from work early, with a hangover, and could see Georgia next door in her front garden peering under a broken flower pot.

Georgia straightened up and accepted.

'Sorry about last night,' said Sally, 'and thanks.'

They often had this sort of exchange. Georgia never knew quite what to say. 'My pleasure', and 'Any time' struck the wrong note. 'It's all right' sounded too much like accepting an apology. So she said, 'They are lovely kids.'

Georgia was one of the women who tended to feel sorry for Beale, albeit Sally was much more of a friend. So, now, accepting her cup of tea, she said, 'It must be hard for Beale, being out of work for so long.'

Sally had been anticipating Georgia saying something pro-Beale, and did not welcome it. 'Yes,' she said rather coldly. What about her own difficulties, as the only bread-winner in the family?

Georgia was not in all contexts a person to spot a fine shade, and went on in the same vein. 'I never forget how marvellous he was in *The Duchess of Malfi.*'

'Five years ago,' said Sally. 'Quite a time. Nothing much since.'

'Unforgettable,' said Georgia, dreamy, impervious. There was a silence, while, looking into space, she remembered.

Sally was afraid Georgia might come out with a quote. 'If you're thinking he must be a wonderful lover, he is,' she said.

Georgia was taken aback, as well she might have been, by this obscure retaliation. The moment it was out of her

30

mouth Sally wished she had not said it. Sally often said things that startled Georgia, so she was not too disconcerted. However, she did say, 'I am sure you know I was thinking no such thing, Sally.'

'Yes, I do, and I am sorry,' said Sally. 'How is the sabbatical going?'

Georgia said that she would be going to the Middle East later in the year, but for the moment, she would be at home, writing, and she was looking forward to it. 'I miss Brenda,' she said. 'Do you?'

Poor, busy, preoccupied Sally did not remember for at least a second who Brenda was. Then she said, 'Yes. Sad not to see her in her study window.'

'I've been wondering whether to write something about her. She didn't have an obituary anywhere.'

'What about "Other Lives" in the *Guardian*? Because she certainly was a character.'

'I think I'm too late for that.'

'Pity.' They were both quiet.

'It seems so strange to me,' said Georgia. 'Not just because Brenda was a wonderful person. I'd feel like this with anyone. There she was, she had her life, and then it was over. She was in her study window, such a familiar sight, and now never again. It makes me wonder, what is a life?'

'Are your parents alive?' asked Sally.

'Both dead,' said Georgia. 'I had this with them. This feeling. It seems to hang a question mark in the air. In the sky.'

'You sweep men away like a dream,' said Sally, whose father, very much alive, was a vicar. 'Like grass which springs up in the morning. In the morning it springs up and flowers, by evening it withers and fades.'

They both laughed a little, each surprised and pleased, even if Georgia did not feel the quotation expressed exactly what she meant. The next moment, they heard a key in the front door. 'Beale,' said Sally. 'Unless one of the kids is out early because it's the first day.' The footsteps went straight upstairs. 'Beale,' said Sally.

Beale it was. He knew Sally was home because he had spotted her car, and his spirits had lifted. Then, entering the house, he heard voices, and could not face a social encounter. He was glad Sally had not seen his suit, and now struggled out of it into his ordinary clothes. He hung up the suit, with the tie, for its next outing. He wondered if Sally was telling a crony about how horrible he was, or how mad. Probably. He was not entirely disappointed not to have got the voice-over. At least he wouldn't have Tally saying, 'Dad, it's your voice, isn't it, in that rubbish ad with a man sitting on a cloud?' But he had been profoundly daunted by the vast number of applicants. Was he ever going to get work again? Perhaps he had better apply for the barista job a coffee shop in the high street was advertising in its window. But what if he didn't get that? He looked in the mirror and ran a hand through his hair. Then he went downstairs, in jeans and a dark blue shirt, not all of its buttons done up, and proceeded to charm Georgia.

~

Eric was waiting outside the school. He began to have a horrible fear that he would not recognise John. Then he remembered about the uniform. John would look different from the others. But Eric need not have worried. John saw him and came straight up to him. They turned to walk home.

'All right first day?' said Eric.

'Yes,' said John.

'Now,' said Eric, 'you must notice the way home.'

'I think I know it,' said John.

'Notice it all the same,' said Eric. 'Another thing I'd like you to notice is glass.'

'What do you mean, glass?'

'How much glass there is in buildings. Not a lot of people realise that. Your school for example. But look at the building ahead. Glass, glass, glass.'

John looked. 'Glass, glass, glass,' he said. 'But why do you like it?'

'I've been in glass all my life,' said Eric.

'In glass?'

'My job.'

They fell silent, but John had been interested. They arrived home. Anne had tea for John spread out on the kitchen table. She gave him a hug.

'First day all right?' she asked.

'Yes,' said John, eating. And in truth it had not been too bad.

'I've got your uniform,' she said. 'There's a lot of it. We'll look at it after tea.' Then she turned to Eric. 'Bad news from Number Five,' she said. 'Maria is in hospital for tests.'

Eric did not like this kind of topic, but Anne was unstoppable. 'She's had a hoarse voice for weeks. I noticed her voice was funny. Different. That's what you need to look out for. Now they think it's cancer of the larynx.'

No answer from Eric. 'Poor Juan,' said Anne. 'I wonder how he'll manage with the children.'

'What is the larynx?' John asked.

Anne turned to him, startled. 'The throat,' she said. 'The vocal cords. What you use to speak. So if the voice gets hoarse it's a bad sign. Did they give you homework, the first day?'

'No. We start homework tomorrow, I think.'

'I've had a text – *Arrived safely in Toronto* – from the family,' Anne told John.

33

'Was it from Mum?'

'Yes.'

'I wonder if she is going to phone me. Did she say?'

'Don't worry if she doesn't for a day or two,' said Anne. 'Think how busy they must be.' John thought. He tried to picture the different members of his family, all busy, in an unimaginable place. His mind evoked Mum's voice. He should never have mentioned her. Now he was going to cry.

'Just got to get to the loo,' he gasped.

Eric had had his eye on John's buttered buns, and now ate one. 'Jolly good tea,' he said. 'Now, is this John's last meal, or does he have supper with us?'

'Let's find out what he would like. You should see the uniform. There's stacks of it. It's draped all over the sitting-room.'

Chapter 4

It had been a cool, sunny day, then a little gentle rain had rustled down at evening, and now it was dusk, and warm. Georgia opened the door on to her garden. She had a torch in her hand. She sat down on the wide and fairly comfortable stone step. However much she learned, knew, wrote and taught about snails, it remained their physical reality that excited her most. And the weather this early September evening spoke to her in a language it does not to most of us.

As she sat, she moved the beam of the torch slowly over the paving stones. And then she saw them. The new hatching. Tiny, perfect snails, each of their shells smaller than a split lentil, were hurrying across the damp stone. Probably it took experience to notice them. People nipping out into their gardens at this hour, to get in the washing, or call the cat, could easily tread unwittingly on a few hundred of them. These snails were too small for their deaths to be signalled by a crunch. Georgia was enthralled, as she regularly was. It was as wonderful as those warm, damp, April evenings, when, sitting on her step, waiting patiently, she heard the waking snails begin to eat. And then, moving the torch, she saw them – the fortunate, or possibly wise, snails that had survived the winter. That was an inspirational moment.

The April event spoke of the restoration of life, of survival, of perseverance, almost of resurrection. Invariably it held Georgia breathless with admiration. These snails had come through, probably in numbers about equal to the many empty shells that lay about them. The September event did not move Georgia to silent applause as did the April one. It was not about courage and recovery. But it was about new and tiny life, and as such it stirred her soul to its depths.

The baby snails were so intrepid and unafraid. They sped along the ground so perfectly. Georgia always wanted to feed them, perhaps with damp porridge oats, but she knew she must not, because it would interfere with Nature. Some of these would have to die, in order that there would be room in her garden for a viable colony. Now she spotted a minute snail which had climbed on to her shoe. She held out her finger to it. Its head waved as it encountered a new dimension. Then it quickly and vigorously scaled Georgia's finger, and she looked closely at it, before placing it with the greatest gentleness on a leaf. For all her knowledge, she had never found out why the newly hatched snails had darker shells than their tabby parents, and bodies of a darker grey.

She checked her shoes and lower legs carefully, then went into the house. She telephoned.

'Harry?' she said.

'Yes,' said Harry's voice.

'It's Georgia. Would you like to come over? The snails have hatched.'

The phone was disconnected with dispatch and there was an almost immediate ring at the doorbell. Georgia and Harry went though to the garden, and together, in awed silence, they sat on the step, Georgia sweeping the path with the torch-beam.

'Do you see them?' Georgia asked. 'I told you it would be soon.'

Harry suddenly did, and his body jerked with delight. 'So tiny,' he said. 'So tiny, but real snails.'

'Exactly.'

'Would it be all right if I picked one up?'

'Better just to watch. They are incredibly fragile at this age.'

They watched. Then, 'There's a shell that isn't moving,' Harry said. 'With no snail.'

'It may have died,' said Georgia. 'It may have dried up somehow. Let's see if we can revive it.'

She stood up carefully, and got a saucer of water from the garden tap. The water was very shallow.

'Pick him up and put him in the saucer,' said Georgia.

Harry picked up the snail with estimable care, and Georgia's practised eye saw that it had withdrawn deep into its shell, presaging death. Harry put the snail into the saucer. Georgia moved the saucer about a bit so that the water almost engulfed the snail. They watched.

'He's moving,' whispered Harry.

Soon a tiny head emerged, and tiny horns unfurled healthily from the head. Georgia bathed the snail a bit more, then placed it on a leaf.

'We brought him back to life,' said Harry.

'Yes, we did. It was you who noticed him.' What is a life? thought Georgia.

'Tons of them must die,' said Harry.

'Oh yes. Tons.'

'Would they be out in our garden?'

'Yes. On an evening like this, they will be hatching in all the gardens.'

'All the gardens in the street?'

'Yes. And everywhere.'

'I'm going to see them in our garden,' said Harry. 'Do you want to come?'

'No, I'll stay here. Watch your feet.'

'Are the ones in our garden legally our snails?'

'I'm afraid I don't know. I doubt if there'd be much competition for them.'

Harry peered closely at his shoes before he left, and Georgia realised with satisfaction that he was not a person she had to exhort to take care.

~

Anne was standing at her gate. She saw Mel Davis approaching.

'How are you, Mel, dear?' asked Anne.

Mel did not really want to stop, but she did, having a few minutes in hand. 'We're okay,' she said.

Anne said, 'Have you heard about Maria?'

'Yes, well, we've heard something. Is it bad?'

'Might or might not be. She's in hospital for tests.'

'I'll call on Juan later and see if there's anything I can do.'

'I've dropped in a chicken casserole.' Anne was always first with the food. 'Juan's very worried.'

'He must be,' said Mel. 'Is your grandson settling in?'

'I hope so. Where are you off to? It's unusual to see you out and about on a weekday.'

Mel did not want to say she had an appointment with the GP to start enquiries about IVF. 'Just a bit of spare time,' she said, and moved on, she hoped not rudely.

That was the trouble with Anne, and that was why some people in the street avoided her, thought Mel. She liked Anne, and was a person who approved in theory of the street being a village. Had Mel been going to Brent Cross, she thought, for something for Hugh's birthday, she would have been delighted to tell Anne. So perhaps it was not fair that today she was irritated by Anne's interest. Anne could not know that her question had touched a sore subject.

Other couples got pregnant. Friends had babies. For most people there seemed to be no problem. Mel passed plenty of prams and buggies, bursting with life, on her short walk to the doctors' surgery. She thought, as she often did, about the trouble she had taken with contraception, in the twelve years since she had become sexually active. And perhaps, all along, she had been infertile. Perhaps she needn't have taken those precautions, nor had those scares that they hadn't worked. She sat down, and began to read an old copy of *Hello!* What was the GP going to say? She and Hugh had been 'trying' for two years. She was twenty-nine and Hugh thirty-two.

It was a disappointing conversation. Dr Meesdon, young, male, and in a hurry, suggested Mel and Hugh wait awhile, say until Mel was thirty. It was a big thing to go into IVF, he said. It messes up your hormones and can leave you broke. Go on leaving it to Nature for the moment, he advised, and come back for a chat if you find you're worrying.

On the way home, Mel wondered about 'if you find you're worrying'. What did he mean? It sounded almost as if he thought that you might switch off having pregnancy and infertility as concerns. The worry might spontaneously pass, as may worries about being in the wrong job, or whether to move to the country. Didn't he realise that it was not a worry that she could ever put out of her mind? She wondered if Dr Meesdon had children. Her picture was that he had, perhaps three, the youngest a baby, all conceived effortlessly. Now, guessed Mel, Mrs Meesdon had gone on the pill, giggling about her and her husband's high degree of fertility. 'We only have to look at each other . . .' Mel decided that next time she would go to another doctor. She and Hugh were never ill, and had only been in the street for two years, so they had not had opportunities to assess the local GP practice which everyone attended. Mel was sure that Anne would have liked to tell her everything about all six of the doctors. For the moment Mel did not want this conversation, though it might be useful some time. Mel took care to turn into the street on the other side of Anne's house; but out of the corner of her eye she saw that Anne was no longer at her gate.

The telephone had called Anne in; it turned out to be Sara. She wanted to speak to John, but had not worked out the time difference correctly, and John was not yet home from school. So Anne and Sara had a chat. Anne was keen for Sara to ring again when John was available, but this did not seem to be an option, given the extreme busyness of Sara's life. So Anne would have to give John messages. How was John? This was a difficult question for Anne, who did not really know the answer, though it was easy enough to say he was all right. He ate his meals, he retired to his attic, he presumably did his homework, and it was understandable that he did not want to spend much of the after-school time in the company of his grandparents. Anne did not want to share doubts and difficulties with Sara, partly so as not to worry her in her busy life, partly so that Sara would think her effortlessly competent. She wanted to hear Sara say, 'Mum, you're marvellous,' and before the end of the conversation Sara did say it.

Sometimes Anne thought she was indeed being marvellous, but at other times she was not so sure. She cooked a good breakfast for John, which he seemed to enjoy. She cooked a high tea for him, a routine which had been decided on in preference to his having supper with Anne and Eric.

Anne did not admit to herself that life had been happier before John. She had been enjoying retirement, with the freedoms it offered her, and with her growing interest in her street. She had immediately agreed to Sara's proposition that John should board with his grandparents, feeling she must. She could not say no to an idea that had so much convenience on its side. But it was not *her* convenience. Her convenience had not been consulted.

And it would have seemed treacherous to raise the possibility that her convenience was not identical to Sara's. That lonely, subversive thought had crept into her mind too late to be of any practical use. When it did appear, she repudiated it. She continued to repudiate it, but more consciously, as time went by, for the disadvantages of having John were more irksome on an everyday basis than they had been in imagination, and imagined advantages failed to materialise. She did not feel at ease with John, as she had expected to, and he did not seem to feel at ease with her. They did not have moments of fun, or growing affection. She fancied that Eric was managing rather better, but Eric, unlike Anne, did not care about being loved.

Anne had never been a person who was thought to be particularly good with children. She had not developed the knack of talking to children in an ordinary way, but tended to make pantomime faces and speak in a special voice. This was actually because children bored her. She and Eric had been well satisfied with one child. Anne had come to feel at ease with Sara in the first few months of Sara's life because Sara was at ease with her. Sara made it clear that Anne was the main person in her life. In spite of this, Anne went back to work as soon as possible, and Sara had a nice minder. But when Sara welcomed Anne with cries and open arms at the end of the working day, Anne went pink with pleasure and enjoyed the physical intensities of motherly love as much as any mother.

Eric did not wonder whether John loved him, nor whether he loved John, nor whether he was conforming to the standard of a proper grandfather. But it was evident to Anne, though not to Eric, who did not think about it, that John preferred Eric to Anne. Anne's conversational efforts towards John did not make him brighten up in the way he had when Eric suddenly said, 'Saturday tomorrow. I'm going to take you to see The Shard. You can have a look at how much glass there is in it.' It had been on the tip of Anne's tongue to say, 'Oh no, Eric, how can you expect John to be interested in that?' But, seeing John's face, she didn't.

She heard John's key in the door, and in a moment he tumbled into the kitchen, covered in his very new grey and maroon uniform. He was holding a copy of a Simpsons magazine. He glanced at Anne and murmured a greeting, and sat down and began to read, his head on his hand.

'Nice day?' asked Anne.

'Okay,' John answered, reading.

'After you left this morning,' said Anne, 'I found your school cap left behind. I hope it didn't matter.'

'No. No one wears those stupid caps.'

John's routine was to sit in the kitchen until his meal appeared, and then to go upstairs. Anne always thought it could be an opportunity for a chat, but it never turned out that way. The glance that he turned on her when he came into the room evinced no interest in or hope for a relationship.

Now Anne said something that she knew would seize his attention. 'Your mother rang.'

John's head came off his hand and he looked directly at her. He was waiting.

'She sent you her love.'

'I thought she was going to ring me this evening. Isn't she going to?'

'She's very sorry, but she can't. It'll be another day.'

John's eyes went back to the magazine, and his hand back to his head. His fingers moved fiercely in his hair. His eyes were blurred with tears.

'Shall I start your supper?' said Anne. Would a proper grandmother put her arms round him, even though he was likely to reject her? She could not risk exposing herself or him to this experiment. It might be an unforgiveable intrusion. So hard to know.

John took a moment to answer. Then he said, 'Yes please.'

~

Beale was waiting for Sally. He had been at home when the children got in from school, and had entertained them while they had their tea. Now Harry was going upstairs to do homework, and Tally preparing to watch a TV programme.

'It's so unfair that I have homework and you don't,' said Harry to Tally.

'The price you pay for the status of secondary school,' said Tally.

'Anyway, you should be doing homework, you're meant to get homework in the top year of primary school.'

'No point when no one marks it.'

'What's yours supposed to be tonight?'

'Write an account of something that happened on the way home from school.'

'What if you get asked to read yours out?'

'I'll make it up as I go along.'

'Pretending to read?'

'If necessary.'

Harry knew that Tally would be able to do this. There was something very clever about Tally. 'You won't get away with that sort of thing at Jibbs,' he said, and they went their different ways.

Beale received a text from Sally. 'Home in 15 hope your there love x.' Beale texted a kiss and put the kettle on.

When Sally walked in, Beale found her as pretty, as mysterious, as watchable, as desirable as he always had. It was partly her clothes, stylish but informal, and usually, as today, with a soft multicoloured scarf somewhere near her face. Beale bought her soft multicoloured scarves whenever he saw any he liked, but the ones she chose for herself were much better. Here she was. She looked so decorative and so capable. Every day she encountered the outside world in a way Beale knew he had never managed to do. She encountered it without faltering, without having to imagine herself in roles in order to enact them, without having to see what someone else thought before giving a view.

'I'm so glad you are the mother of my children,' he said. 'You'll counteract me in them.'

She wasn't listening, but glancing at a pile of letters. Abstraction was part of her charm.

'Cup of tea,' said Beale, and this time she did hear, came into the room properly, kissed Beale and sat down.

'Okay day?' he asked.

She told him one or two troublesome things and some welcome ones, and took her shoes off. 'Kids home?' she asked.

That was another difference between Beale and Sally, he thought. He always checked on the kids immediately, fearing accidents. She did not have to. Now he went for the more comfortable pair of shoes she changed into at this time of day, and stooped in front of her to put them on her feet. He kissed an elegant knee.

'You're very nice,' she said. She buried her hands gently in his thick hair.

'Sometimes. Do you have to work tonight?'

'About two hours. Plus seven phone calls. No, eight.'

'I'll get supper.'

'I'll have to have it working, I'm afraid.'

Beale sighed. Then he said, 'We can have precious moments now.' He picked up the paper and turned to the easy crossword. It was half done.

'The easy crossword is half done,' he said, incredulously.

'Oh yes. I was waiting for a phone call this morning to hear where a meeting was. So I had a look at it, and it rather ran away with me.'

'What?'

'Sorry.'

'I can't believe this. We just said it was something we were always going to do together.'

'Sorry.'

'Yes, but we just said we were going to do it together, and then you do it by yourself. Did you even think, when you were doing it, that we had said that? Just yesterday?'

'I don't know, don't make a thing of it.'

'Make a thing? It *is* a thing. You don't care whether you do things with me or not. That's the meaning of it.'

'It isn't.'

'It is. We say we'll do the crossword together, and you do it by yourself –'

'Not all of it.'

'– and you don't care whether we have supper together or not.'

'I do, but I have to get this work done tonight.'

'It's your utter indifference to me that hurts.'

'I have to work hard because I'm the only one bringing in money.'

This was easily said, and gave Sally a very solid leg to stand on. But the fact was that, as she fiddled with the crossword this morning, she had *not* forgotten the undertaking they had made that every day they would do it amicably together, perhaps at about this time. She had remembered it. She knew she was playing with fire. Why had she done it? She didn't know.

'You're punishing me,' he said, 'for not being able to get work.'

'I think it's more because, well, if we are reduced to doing

45

the *Guardian* easy crossword together to feel close, where are we?'

'That's not the only way we feel close,' said Beale, after a minute.

Now Sally too thought of sex. There was a short silence. Then, 'It's a pity we drink so much,' said Sally.

'I know. Sometimes in the morning I can hardly remember sex.' He did not add that he racked his memory even for whether it had happened or not. 'Shall we try and drink less?'

'What would less be?

'One bottle of wine at supper. But that would be too little, and anyway it seems we don't have supper.'

'Do you mean one bottle each?'

'No.'

'Just one bottle.'

'Yes. I know it sounds silly.'

Both were thinking that somehow they had avoided a quarrel. The combustible material had been there, but had not blazed. Both were pleased. 'I'll start your supper,' said Beale, 'for you to eat at your computer. While I eat mine watching *Celebrity Big Brother*. Such is life.'

Chapter 5

Georgia had lived alone since a relationship finished ten years ago. That was when she moved into the street. She had no children. She was fifty-nine.

She found she preferred being on her own, and perhaps that quality in her was one of the reasons why the relationship had come to an end. Perhaps it was also a reason why the ending had not been acrimonious.

She was enjoying her sabbatical. It was not as productive so far as she had expected, but then she had not expected Brenda to die. There were some research papers she wanted to write before she went on her travels. She was behind with those. It didn't matter. The major paper would be written when she returned from Egypt, her brain teeming with new insights and understandings.

The nieces appeared to have let Brenda's house. The For Sale notice remained in place outside, but there were residents. They were temporary. Anne had discovered from them that they were leaving at Christmas. Georgia watched them. They were never to be seen in Brenda's study, towards the window of which Georgia's eyes had traditionally always been drawn. Perhaps Brenda's study was not involved in the let, or perhaps, understandably, the tenants did not like it. The big front room on the first floor, Brenda's dusty and unused sitting-room,

47

was their living area. The window of that room was almost always open now, and a young woman with long dark hair would sit on the sill, half in and half out of the house, and smoke a cigarette. The young man could be seen in the distance, through the glass, moving about. Perhaps he did not smoke. If he had smoked, the woman's smoke might not have had to have been so scrupulously exiled. Would they stay together? wondered Georgia. Would each remember these few months in Palmerston Street all their lives? There were always big vases of flowers within reach of the window. Georgia could not see what the flowers were, but would the smell of some of them, arrived at unexpectedly, in fifty years, evoke these months? Sometimes the young woman would dry her hair as she sat on the window sill, and she brushed it as it dried, and at some point lit a cigarette.

A small snail had made its way to the side of Georgia's window, decided injudiciously to stick there, and had cooked in the September sun. Georgia saw at a glance that it had died, for the shell was translucent. She wished she had spotted it in time. Georgia enjoyed rescue more than anything – more than success, in so far as she was acquainted with it; more than friendship; more than eating; more than sex. Her love of snails had begun with rescue. Her mother had a vegetable patch, and Georgia became aware that there was a war on snails. There was a vat of salty water and into this her gardening mother would throw snails as she found them. It smelt terrible. 'What's this?' Georgia, aged four, asked her mother, and it was explained. Georgia started collecting snails to keep them safe. She housed them under basins, flower pots with a stone on top, an up-ended aquarium. Her mother was not uncooperative; as long as the snails were off her garden, that was all she wanted. Georgia tended her snails, fed them with dandelion and other leaves, and watched them. Once, replacing the heavy aquarium, she crushed a snail. It was Derek. If she was honest, she had never got over it.

Still looking out into the street, and drawn by the blank window of Brenda's study, by the empty snail shell, and by the ephemeral couple opposite Georgia thought yet again, 'What is a life?' Georgia saw Juan come out of his house with one of his children. Her heart sank for that little family, of which Maria was the life and soul. Now that she could be sure Juan was out, she thought she could leave a get well card and perhaps a box of eggs on the front step. Would a box of eggs be appropriate? Georgia's informant was Anne, and Anne seemed drawn to gloom about hospital outcomes. For all anybody knew, Maria might be going to be all right.

~

John trained Benn to come up the ladder to his attic. It was not so difficult as Benn had expected, though he found it hard to do it gracefully. Going down was worse, though he had also mastered that. So Benn might sit and purr on John's futon while John was doing his homework, or look out of the skylight at passing birds, or even try to walk on the computer.

John settled into school work, and did not find it difficult. At home there were no distractions. He did not have a TV in his attic and did not want to watch the one in the sitting-room. At school he had managed to fit in, though he had not made friends yet, at least, not friends who invited him to their houses or to football after school. But there were people he could have a bit of a laugh with, and his northern accent could catch their attention and amuse them. Most classmates were part of a phalanx of friends from local primary schools, so they already had a group to belong to. John was an outsider, but was not picked on. Jibbs was not, or not at that point, a school at which it was ridiculous to be clever or contemptible to keep in with the teachers. John was managing.

He spent more time in his attic than he needed for home-work, though his grandparents did not know this. There was Benn, and sometimes John buried his face in Benn's soft fur, usually his tummy, and the tears came. When Benn was else-where, John might climb on to the desk and carefully open a skylight. He would put his head out, and feel near the sky and the clouds. He had started bringing up crumbs or pieces of bread after tea and feeding the pigeons. They had quickly got the idea, and when his head popped out of the roof there was the sound of beating wings and a score of beautiful pigeons landed on the tiles to jerk and peck. This made John very happy. At other times he could get absorbed in computer games, or games on his mobile phone. Sometimes he glanced at the books Eric had installed for him. None of them were very attractive to the eye, but he had a go at *Treasure Island*, and told Eric he was reading it, though actually he had got stuck and put it aside. This led to a few abortive conversational sallies from Eric.

'Leave him,' said Anne to Eric, after one such. 'He's obviously not reading it. They don't, these days.'

'What do they read?'

'That magazine he brought in, I suppose.'

'That can't be all.'

'No. He must be reading a book at school. For English. But he doesn't really answer when I ask him.'

'He might like *David Copperfield*.'

'I don't think so.'

But Eric had been thinking of David's walk to Dover, undertaken when he was ten, a year younger than John. Eric was vaguely aware that what John was going through was an ordeal, and wondered whether it might help him if he could know that people of his age clenched their teeth and came through worse ordeals than this.

~

Hugh Davis wanted to put it from his mind that Mel was going to the doctor to ask about IVF. He had attempted to dissuade her.

'No need to go yet. We're too young. People start that in their mid-thirties.'

'Well, but I want to go.'

'Why?'

'We've had unprotected intercourse for two years. Something must be wrong.'

'Not necessarily. It's a hit and miss business.'

'Not usually that hit and miss.'

This was true enough to silence Hugh.

'If there's something wrong with me,' Mel went on, 'quite likely it could be fixed. If it's fixed before I'm thirty, we'd be ahead of the game.'

'And if it can't be fixed,' said Hugh, thinking, 'wouldn't you rather not know for a few more years?'

Mel took her eyes off her coffee cup and looked straight at Hugh, troubled and annoyed. 'If I'd seen more TV dramas,' she said, ' I'd say I can't believe you said that.'

'Sorry. I was stupid.'

'It's always better to know things.'

Hugh could not bring himself to agree with this, but did not dare disagree. Mel took his silence for assent.

Hugh was relieved and a little triumphant when Mel told him what Dr Meesdon had said. 'Basically he agrees with me,' Hugh said. 'You're worrying too soon.' However, 'Wait until you are thirty' resounded rather unpleasantly in his ears, for that would be Mel's next birthday. This was only a reprieve.

'I'm worried I'm not enjoying sex,' said Mel. 'I find myself thinking let's wait a few days until the optimum time. Then when we have sex I find myself thinking is this fuck the one. Then I think because I'm anxious and conscious that'll militate against conception, so I worry more.'

'Try to forget all about it,' said Hugh.

'Easily said.' Mel knew this was a problem for her in a way it was not a problem for Hugh. Hugh didn't mind if he didn't have a baby, and only had parental yearnings on Mel's behalf. 'I'm glad you don't mind either way,' she said. 'That makes it easier for me. If you were broody too, it would be awful.'

'Good,' said Hugh. 'I'm not in the least broody. Now, back to important things. What shall we have for supper?'

~

Mel's worry was out in the open, and they both knew exactly what it was, though Hugh did not always bear in mind its all-pervasive character. Hugh's worry was secret.

Three years before he met Mel, a lesbian friend asked him for sperm. He agreed. She wanted it done properly, so Hugh had a sperm test, while she got checked out for anything obviously wrong. This venture came to nothing, in the event, for Min and Terry changed their minds about wanting a baby, and, indeed, split up. The idea of a baby, Min told Hugh afterwards, had been a last attempt to keep the relationship afloat. It had failed. The legacy of it for Min was a clean bill of health as far as fertility was concerned. The legacy for Hugh was anxiety and regret, anger that he had airily agreed to be tested, and something of a cloud under which he had to live.

His strategy was to try to forget what had happened, and this had been successful, to the extent that as his relationship with Mel began and developed, he did not think about his sperm count. It did not come into his mind. The happy days in which he met Mel, and they fell in love and became partners, then got married, and bought and did up a house in the street; those happy days were unmarked and unhaunted by the vague memory of that depressing report. For it had been depressing. His sperm were much fewer than average per quantity of seminal fluid, and for the most part, lacked motility. Why motility? Why not mobility? The peculiar word motility whispered within him and had been hard to shake off. But his mind was wiped clean of it once he was with Mel. By then the sperm count felt like a bad dream from long ago, and if he thought about it at all, it was with a certain derision. Because of Mel, his confidence in himself as a man was flying high. The report was probably mistaken, or had caught his sperm at a low moment. He was very glad that he had told no one. No one knew, not even Min, and that made the episode easier to eliminate.

He had not expected Mel to be so determined to have a baby. He had not foreseen that she would want to go for it the minute they moved into their house. But she was, and she did. And in two years, nothing had happened.

Now that Mel was bringing in the medical profession, Hugh was increasingly uncomfortable. It was not so much that he was afraid he would eventually be called on for a sperm test, which, of course, he would, eventually. And if the results were the same as last time, it would be horrible, horrible both for him and for Mel. That scenario was hard, but bearable. Worse was the fact that he was deceiving Mel. He was living a lie. The result of the sperm test, when it came, would be a bombshell for Mel, and he would have to pretend it was equally a bomb-shell for him. What else could he do? Regrets fidgeted in his mind. If only he had said no to Min and Terry. His stupid yes to them had been said with a boyish phallic swagger he now utterly despised. Or if only Min and Terry had broken up a few weeks earlier. Then this unwanted knowledge would not have been there to plant itself in his memory, and there would have been no deception of Mel. Or, if only he had confessed to Mel, as they got serious, that this skeleton sat in his cupboard. But he knew he could not have done that. She might have left him. Sometimes, when he saw Mel worrying, he would say, light-heartedly, feigning the innocence he longed for, 'It may just as well be me, you know.' But he could see she didn't believe him, and his male pride was gratified by her disbelief.

And now, sex was becoming a problem. Not a problem; Hugh resisted that word, and so did Mel. But sex was contaminated. On Mel's side, as she had said, the sense of calculation and failure had begun to obtrude. The difficulties on Hugh's side could not be talked about, for they belonged to his secret. He was becoming daily more aware of his deception, and felt more and more stuck in it as time went by. Also, instead of feeling at ease and at one with his sperm, he was consciously critical of it. He did not want to produce spermatazoa with low motility, and too few of them at that. He wanted huge crowds of them, lashing their tails, each determined to be the winner. He began to look at other men, and envied their imagined plenty.

He was so used to putting his arms round Mel in bed and beginning to make love to her. This impulse had not been blighted.

'Let's wait a couple of days,' whispered Mel, who had recently invested in an ovulation predictor.

'Why? We can make love now, *and* in a couple of days.'

'But the fertility book says sperm are at their best after a few days' build-up.'

Hugh rolled away, unhappy. He stared at the ceiling.

'I'm sorry to make it all so . . .' said Mel. She could not find a word for what she was making it.

~

Sally Pace also had a guilty secret. She was carrying about in her handbag a cheque for £5000. She suspected it was ill-gotten.

Able, willing, easy on the eye, experienced, unflappable and extremely pleasant, Sally got on well at work. No one was more conscious of her attractive qualities than her line manager, Ron. They had developed a flirtatious relationship, its banter often quite public; but at office parties and other occasions when the drink flowed, Ron had showed he hoped for more. So far, Sally had managed to keep things nice while she turned him down, but she was not quite at ease at those moments, and, on the whole, she wished she hadn't slipped quite so far into the verbal intimacies which he hoped would lead further. Sometimes this was rather worrying, because she didn't want to endanger her very good job.

The previous June, Sally came in for a bonus of £5000. This had been useful for the family holiday, and had helped with the mortgage. Beale had been delighted, and had felt rich, and together they went on a clothes shopping spree; but, actually, the money had not amounted to much. There were debts on Sally's credit card; there was the new car Sally wanted. The bonus was long exhausted before these outlays could be considered.

She talked to Ron, by way of joking, about how the bonus had dwindled to nothing. He joked back, but after a few days ago a cheque was laid on the keyboard of her computer as she worked.

'What's this for?'

'It's a second bonus.'

'But it's signed by you. It's your cheque.' She looked up at him, and could not prevent wide eyes and a beguiling expression.

'I'll get it back, don't worry.'

'Oh no. I know I'm your treasure and your irreplaceable one. Knowing that is bonus enough.'

'Look, I'm serious,' said Ron. 'Put it towards the car. You've earned it.'

'I'll tear it up, of course,' said Sally.

'Do what you like with it, darling. It's yours. Don't mention it again, please.' He kissed the top of her head.

Sally had not torn up the cheque, and had not taken it out of her handbag.

She was shocked that her feelings told her she was in a dilemma. How could it be a dilemma? She knew exactly what she should do. But somehow she could not do it, or hadn't done it yet. Her mind insisted on playing with the possibility of not tearing up the cheque. That also presented dilemmas, ones which she could not stop herself from visiting. She couldn't put the cheque into the bank account, or Beale would certainly ask about it. Easygoing in many ways, he kept a keen and fussy eye on their bank statements, probably hoping against hope to recognise some money earned by him. She couldn't pretend it was another bonus, because she had received one so recently. It would be safer and simpler, as well as right, to destroy the cheque.

What had Ron meant about 'I'll get it back'? she wondered. Perhaps he intended to claim some expenses that would cover it. That was quite likely, as he was always claiming expenses, and in that case it would not be wrong for her to accept it. Or not more wrong than a lot of things that happen all the time. She had tried to speak with him about it, but he was adamant. Not a word would he say, or hear.

Then there was 'You've earned it.' This made Sally think of all the extra and unpaid work she had done for Ron over time. She had always felt it was part of the job, or possibly part of the friendship. But maybe he was seeking a way graciously to reimburse her for her time and trouble. The cheque could be covert wages, not gratuity. Might she think of it like that?

But what if it was a bribe? Would the moment she slipped from his clutches with a light laugh at the next office party be more difficult if the sum of £5000 were to be present in her mind – or, worse, in his? Or in both, simultaneously? And would she perhaps see it glinting in his eye, firming his resolve, putting her morally in the wrong for refusing? She quailed at this scenario, and did her best to dismiss it.

She found that she could not easily bear to relinquish the £5000. Ten thousand would have been too much; two, too little, and a cheque for either she could have righteously declined. She found herself smiling when she thought about the money. She felt glee on her face. It offered so many possibilities, including the car. And, she thought, it was no more than her deserts, in a way, because of Beale earning nothing. She decided at least to bank the cheque, which committed her to nothing.

She had never had a secret from Beale before, and it was uncomfortable. Of course she had practised small deceptions, like the price of a coat, or whether she had spent the evening complaining about him to a friend. But this was different. This was something big. What would happen, she wondered, if she told him? She couldn't make up her mind whether he would say something more like 'Don't look a gift horse in the mouth, take the silly bugger's cheque, we need the money', or something more like 'Burn the cheque this minute, you shameless prostitute!' Either response would rob her of the freedom of her own decision.

Chapter 6

John was standing on his desk, throwing crumbs for the pigeons through the skylight, when his mobile rang. He jumped down, and groped for it in the pocket of his blazer which dangled from the back of the chair. It was his mother.

'At last I've got you,' she said. 'I've been trying and trying to ring you. Now, darling, how are you?'

It was the sound of her voice, so utterly itself, unmistakeable when heard, unimaginable when hearkened for in his mind, that brought him close to tears.

'Okay,' he said.

'I haven't managed to get you on the phone, but I've left you lots of messages with Granny. I hope she's passed them on.'

'Yes, she has.'

'How is school?'

'Okay.'

'Tell me three things about it.'

Three things. That was so like Mum. John cleared his throat. 'Our form teacher is called Mr Mann.'

'That's one.'

'There are stick insects in the lab.'

'What? What insects?'

'Stick insects.'

'I could hardly hear you. What's number three?'

'I hate French.'

'Talk louder, your voice sounds so different, I can't understand what you're saying.'

John gripped his neck with his other hand, because his throat was hurting from trying not to cry. 'French is my worst subject.'

'Are you playing football?'

'Yes.'

'Are you all right?'

'What do you mean, all right?'

'Your voice sounds very funny. What's happened to it?'

John was silent.

'Your voice is different.' Now he heard his mother talking over her shoulder to someone else, probably Dad. She turned back to the phone. 'It's awful, but I'll have to go. Sorry, darling, speak soon.' And she rang off. So did John.

His heart was pounding and there was sweat on his forehead. He was recapitulating what his mother had said. She had told him his voice sounded different. His voice sounded funny. He gasped with fear. It must be cancer of the larynx.

This horrifying realisation outweighed the pleasure or the pain that would otherwise have attended the longed-for conversation. He cleared his throat a few times. Then he said, 'Hey, good idea, cool,' as something to say, while he listened to his voice. He could not tell if it sounded funny or not, but he thought it did. His mum knew his voice, and to her it sounded funny, and different. Those were just the symptoms Granny had said you must look out for. It was cancer. He would certainly die.

He heard a very distant ring on the doorbell, and then Eric was coming up the stairs. 'It's Tallulah Pace,' he called from the landing, panting slightly. 'She's come to visit you.' And Tally Pace came up the ladder and into the attic. 'Hi,' she said.

'Hi.' John's acquaintance with the Pace children had been sponsored by Anne, and he wasn't sure whether they liked him or not. They had only met a couple of times. Once Anne had had Harry and Tally to tea, and after Anne's delicious lasagne and cake the children fell back on watching TV. The second time Harry and John had walked home from school together, and had met up with Tally in the street, and the three of them had seen how far each could kick a Coca Cola can. That had been fun. But John was surprised to see Tally in his attic, at a moment when he was still reeling from the diagnosis of mortal illness.

'Wow,' said Tally. 'Look at this. Lucky!' She looked all round the room. She looked at the skylights. 'Lucky, lucky,' she said. 'You should see our bedrooms.' Tallulah Pace, aged ten, was slim, elegant and blonde. John thought she was very beautiful. He wanted to say, 'Has my voice gone funny?' But of course he couldn't. He was afraid of speaking at all, in case she said, 'Wow, your voice is funny, what's the matter with you?'

The skylight was still open. 'Can we look out of the roof window?' she said.

'We have to get on the desk,' said John. She did not look shocked by the sound of his voice, and he was encouraged. Shoulder to shoulder, they looked out of the skylight. 'The sky is so near,' said Tally, awed and almost whispering. 'Are those the roofs of the houses on the other side of the street?'

'Yes,' said John. 'And you can see into their attic windows, if you stand on your toes. Look.'

'Whose house is that one opposite?'

'I'm afraid I don't know. I can find out.'

'Do you spy on them? Oh look, the pigeons.' For the pigeons, of course, had come back, spotting human heads at the skylight, and hoping for a second helping. 'The pigeons. You lucky,

lucky . . . You can almost touch them.' She reached a hand out, and a pigeon purred and edged away.

John was happy that his quarters were admired by Tally. 'It's a great attic,' he said. Her face expressed no surprise at the timbre of his voice. Was she just being polite?

'You could feed them,' she said.

'I do.'

'Have you got anything?'

'No, it's used up.'

'Can I bring some birdseed round?'

'Yes.'

'Oh I forgot, Dad wants you to come to tea tomorrow. But it's much better here. Our house is rubbish.'

John did not know what to say to this. He conjectured that Tally did not know his voice well enough to register that it had gone funny. He was pretty sure he was dying, but he noticed that he felt much better since she had come into the room. He was glad she liked it so much, and that she would come again, with birdseed.

∼

'Tally says can I go to tea tomorrow,' John whispered, later.

Anne looked up. She was doing her patchwork. Her glasses were on the end of her nose, which John always liked. 'Have you got a sore throat?' she asked. 'You're whispering.'

'Sorry,' said John, shamed into risking his normal voice.

'Of course you can go to tea with the Paces tomorrow. Is your throat all right?'

That John could not answer. But he had another question. 'Who lives at Number Twenty-three, just opposite us?'

Anne was pleased by 'us', and smiled. Then she said, 'They are French students. Three of them. One of them is called Jean-Luc. I should get to know them better.'

John began to withdraw. 'Won't you stay down here, darling?' said Anne. 'It's jollier. Eric will be back in a moment. He's just shopping.'

John hesitated. 'No, I just have to . . .' He was gone.

Eric came home with the shopping, and found places for his purchases in the kitchen. Then he went to put away some computer paper which, to his pleased surprise, he had been able to buy at the supermarket. Having done that, he came downstairs.

'What's up with John, do you know?' he asked.

'Up with him?' Poor Anne looked up, startled.

'He's reciting.'

'Reciting?' She put down her needle.

They crept upstairs together to the landing beneath the attic. They could hear John. They could not make out the words, but the rhythm told them he was reciting poems.

'What ever?' whispered Eric.

'It must be for school,' said Anne. 'Maybe they have to learn . . .'

'I didn't think schools did that any more.'

They listened. There was a curious intensity in the tone. Then they heard John clear his throat and start again. 'Oh dear,' said Anne. Anne and Eric went downstairs. They were both mystified, but they were trying to normalise in their minds what they had heard. After all, it was not so strange.

'Has he seemed funny?' Eric asked. 'Earlier?'

'I thought he might have a bit of a throat.'

～

In his attic, with quiet determination, John was listening to his voice. He was trying to tell whether it sounded different, funny, or hoarse. He had never listened to his voice before.

So it was hard to be sure. Sometimes he thought it was all right; sometimes he detected a possible huskiness. He had run out of the things he could think of to say, so had pulled a book from the shelves. He opened it anywhere, and read aloud.

> *Under the wide and starry sky*
> *Dig the grave and let me lie.*
> *Glad did I live and gladly die,*
> *And I lay me down with a will.*
>
> *This be the verse you grave for me:*
> *Here he lies, where he longed to be.*
> *Home is the sailor, home from the sea,*
> *And the hunter, home from the hill.*

He read it again and again, trying to monitor the sound of his voice, sometimes optimistic, more often dashed. In the end he put down the book, for he knew the poem by heart. The poem helped him. The poet was brave about his death. He looked forward to it, in a way. He was homesick for it. It was home, to him. Perhaps, John thought, listening carefully to his voice's every inflection, and full of mortal foreboding, perhaps he could learn to feel the same.

In the course of time John was to become a sound engineer, and, all his life, whenever he needed to use his voice to test levels and acoustics, it was lines from this poem that he spoke.

~

Later that evening Georgia dropped in on Anne and Eric. She did this quite often now, she hoped not too often. An excuse had been that she was helping Benn settle in, but that was a thin excuse now, as he was so obviously well settled. Did Eric say, ' Why is that Georgia of yours always coming round?' Or did he by any chance say, 'It's rather nice seeing more of Georgia Fox'?

It was because of the sabbatical that she had so many spare hours. She could not remember when in adulthood she had felt as leisured as she did now. Certainly not in holiday periods, for then she was obliged to pack and hurry off somewhere. This pensive mood had started with the death of Brenda. Georgia did not shake off Brenda's death, nor did she want to. Everybody should be mourned by someone. Georgia did not exactly think about Brenda. She had done all the remem-berings she could do, and did not know how to think further. It was more like when elephants revisit the place where a fellow elephant has died, and stand there for a while, trunks swaying. Georgia went regularly to the place in her mind where Brenda had died. She stood there.

Meanwhile she was becoming very fond of Anne Darwin. She was not sure how this had crept up on her. Their acquaint-ance had become friendship at the time of Brenda's death. They had sought and found the crematorium together in Georgia's car, Anne clutching the map, and together they had organised the re-homing of Benn. There had been some laughs. Then Georgia had developed a bad cold, and Anne appeared on her doorstep with vegetable soup. Georgia offered to child-sit for the Darwins, and was invited to meet John. She talked interestingly to him about snails over high tea, and introduced him to the notion of hermaphroditism. Anne thought this a bit daring, but conceded in her mind that it was very discreetly done. Afterwards, when John had disappeared, in mock but real distress Anne raised the question of why other people were more successful with John than she was. Georgia listened sympathetically, then suggested that John might be angry about being left, and might be taking it out on his grandmother.

This had never occurred to Anne, who thought about things in quite a different way. It suggested to her that Georgia might have been in psychotherapy, and this she nerved herself to ask. Georgia welcomed the question, reassuring the diffidence with which it was put, and said that indeed she had been in psychotherapy, fifteen years ago for five years.

These topics fostered intimacy. But the level of growing friendship did not explain, thought Georgia, why Anne had become an object of excitement to her. Not only pleasure and interest, but actual excitement. Georgia recognised in herself a slight crush on Anne one warm night as she strolled home from a visit to the Darwins. Anne had invited her to watch a DVD of *The Iron Lady* with her and Eric. It had been an enjoyable evening. Anne and Georgia had been disrespectful and giggly, and Eric, not that he was right-wing, but because a film should be uninterrupted by chat, had drawn the two of them together by his attempts to shut them up. But Georgia identified the new feeling as having begun not during the film, but when she arrived at the house, and, let in by Eric, surprised Anne at her patchwork. The coloured squares, invisibly sewn together, lay over Anne's lap and cascaded on to the floor. More squares were in a wicker basket at Anne's side. When Georgia came in, Anne began to gather the material to put it away, looking up at Georgia over her glasses with a warm smile. 'Oh please don't,' said Georgia. 'Let me see it, it's so beautiful.'

Thus they talked about patchwork while they looked at it together, and Georgia knelt and and held a swathe in both hands, studying it, clamouring to know when and why Anne had learned to do it, and marvelling at how difficult it must be; and Anne spoke of her grandmother and an aunt, and Georgia said how much she wished she could do it herself, but it was too late now, and Anne demurred about its difficulty and about its being too late for Georgia, though of course it was. As Georgia walked home, she realised it was this event that had added excitement to the feelings she already had for Anne.

Georgia had not identified as a lesbian in a spirit of feminist principle or gay pride. She had just gradually noticed that, unlike contemporaries of her gender, she did not move from a crush on the art teacher to interest in boys, nor even from a crush on the art teacher to a crush on the metalwork teacher. She had remained a person for whom hero-worship was the portal to love, and her hero-worship was always for those of her own sex. Why was her heart moving in this familiar direction towards Anne? she wondered. She realised she found Anne beautiful, though she was not sure she always had. She did now. She was moved by Anne's thinness, by her shapeless cardigan pulled double across her front against the cold, by her craggy face, by her determined walk, by her neglected hair, by the surprisingly resonant chuckle that was her laugh. She was moved by Anne's unconsciousness of the fact that anyone could be viewing her as an object of emotional curiosity or delight. It must have been a long time, thought Georgia, since Eric had seen her as anything other than the outward sign of whatever it was that he needed her to mean. That was no different from how Anne looked at Eric; but Georgia found it easy to persuade herself that Eric had started it. Georgia felt that whereas Eric had become genuinely indifferent, Anne had undergone a loss of hope, stoically borne, and, over years, that she had been ground down by it.

~

But Georgia had despaired too easily of Eric, as people are inclined to do when addressing themselves to the rescue of the other partner. Eric might not have been in the habit of noticing Anne, but he certainly began to notice the way Georgia looked at her.

'Well, you've definitely got a fan,' said Eric, pensively, at the sink, where he was washing up.

'What do you mean?' Anne asked. The other sort of fan had come to mind, and she was puzzled.

'Georgia Fox thinks the world of you.'

'Georgia thinks . . .' Anne's tone was incredulous and she did not finish her sentence. She was pink and smiley at what was evidently a new idea.

Eric turned round and looked at Anne. His face relaxed into what was his nicest smile, affectionate and rueful, perhaps wise. He realised he had not seen exactly that sparkle in Anne's eyes for many years.

'Well, and I like her too,' said Anne. 'It's mutual. We have been friends ever since Brenda died.' She had an itch to render the relationship ordinary in her own eyes and in Eric's.

Eric continued to look at Anne for another minute. He felt unusually light-hearted. It was as if an art expert had visited his house and said that a picture which had been hanging disregarded on the wall for fifty years might be an original. 'You are a dear,' he said. 'Do you ever feel I don't pay enough attention to you?'

'No, of course I don't,' Anne said instantly. 'Good heavens. We're seventy.'

'You aren't, yet.'

'Near enough. What would I do with attention?'

'You are getting it from Georgia.'

'Nonsense. Anyway, she comes round to help with the cat.'

'I don't see what help we need with the cat, and in fact she never sees him, now that he spends most of his time upstairs in John's room.'

'You do like Georgia, don't you?'

'Yes.' This was true. Eric always warmed to erudition, even when it was about snails. And Georgia was always happy to hear from him about glass, or the pains of retirement.

'Good.' Anne turned her attention back to rolling out pastry for the steak and kidney pie, a favourite with both John and Eric.

Chapter 7

Mel was taking another morning off work. This time she did not tell Hugh. He always left the house half an hour before she did, so he was unaware of any change of routine. Anne was nowhere to be seen as Mel passed her house, for which Mel was grateful. This was Mel's first venture into private medicine, and privileging herself in this way was enough to make her feel guilty, even if she had not been, for the first time, doing something behind Hugh's back.

But at the end of the long morning, she was glad she had done it. She had to go straight to work from the private clinic, so busyness at work made it hard to rejoice with her whole heart. It was only when she got home and stood looking out of the window with a cup of tea in her hands, ready to unpack and enjoy her happiness, that the happiness became ambiguous, as happiness is so prone to do.

The nice gynaecologist had examined her carefully and asked her a number of questions. There had been blood tests and other tests, some a bit painful. Some of the results could not be revealed immediately, but a letter would be sent itemising all the findings. Nothing unpleasant was to be expected in this letter. The very experienced and rather well-known clinician in whose hands she was, and who had been recommended by a medical friend, said that everything in Mel's reproductive system was normal and healthy and there was no reason why she should not conceive.

As Mel started sipping her tea, she was smiling broadly. She could not stop smiling. She loved her body again, her body which was proven to be ordinary and wonderful. In recent months – perhaps, indeed, for over a year – she had come to suspect and mistrust her body, and to feel betrayed by it. Now she was overwhelmed by a sense of recovered female potency, unmerited and miraculous but, for the majority of women, and herself in the past, taken for granted. Motherhood was not denied her, as she had gradually come to fear that it would be. Indeed her relief had two dimensions. The predominant one for the moment was about herself and her glorious body. Behind that was another, which was about the baby she could have, the baby that would be hers and Hugh's.

Before she had finished her tea, disturbing ideas intruded. Given that there was nothing wrong with her, could it be that Hugh was infertile? She had never seriously entertained this idea, regarding Hugh's references to it as a kind of joke. The terrible thought ran its course through her mind. What if he was? Two years was quite a long time. What if he could not get her pregnant? Ever? And he, who was so at ease with sex, always ready for it, priding himself on his horniness – it seemed so unlikely that it was him. But it had to be a possibility, given what she had found out today. For a moment, she even wished that the gynaecologist's verdict had gone the other way. Better that she should deal with such a body blow than that he should have to. What would it do to him? She would have to ask him to have a sperm test. He would be humiliated. Their sex life was already challenged by her tiresome familiarity with her reproductive cycle, but this would make it much worse. Much, much worse.

She heard Hugh's key in the front door. He always called her name as he came in to the house.

'Kitchen,' Mel shouted back, and Hugh appeared, smiling, happy to see her, his hair tousled by the bike helmet he had just pulled off, his rucksack still on his shoulders.

'Good,' he said. 'I was afraid you mightn't be back.' He came forward to hug her, but then stopped, looking into her face. 'What's the matter?' he asked. 'You're all pale and . . . What's the matter?'

So Mel had to tell him. The fact that she had bypassed the GPs and the NHS, going against Hugh's principles as much as her own, was as nothing now, and it was even as nothing that she had been concealing her project from him. He felt both as muffled, passing blows, and waited, painfully, for the end of the story. They remained standing, Hugh holding Mel under her elbows, each looking intently into the other's face.

'Okay,' he said when she finished. 'Good. I'm glad you've had this reassurance. So shall we just leave it for a while, as the GP said we should?'

They sat down on kitchen chairs, their knees touching. Mel was relieved to have come out with everything; Hugh was in a panic, and groping for a strategy.

'I'd rather go on trying to sort things out,' said Mel. 'Would you go for a sperm test? They do them in the clinic I went to this morning.'

'Yes, all right,' said Hugh. Was there anything else he could say?

Mel's tense expression relaxed into a smile. 'Oh good,' she said. 'I was afraid you wouldn't want to.'

'Why wouldn't I?'

'Oh, I don't know. Male pride?'

'Well, I admit I don't want to.' Hugh was glad to be able to say that much truthfully. 'I don't want to but I will.'

'Thank you.' Mel was thinking how she could minimise the

annoyance for him. She could be the one to phone to make the appointment. She could fit it in Hugh's lunch-hour.

They cooked, and opened a bottle of wine. There was a football match which they had planned to watch. They ate in front of the TV. If Mel noticed that Hugh's spirits were crushed, she put it down at first to the exigencies of male pride, and then to the fact that England was not winning. She had regained a version of happiness – not the earlier euphoria attendant on contemplation of her perfect self, but a more prosaic sense that the matter was now properly in hand. The worry about how they would cope if Hugh's sperm was amiss was there, but in abeyance. She could not believe it of him, and, anyway, he appeared unconcerned.

Hugh hoped that Mel would attribute what he thought was his obvious misery throughout the evening to his reluctance, nobly overcome, to starting a family so soon. That would be a normal, fairly grown up attitude for a man. But his real state of mind was far removed from that. He was shocked and horrified at the hole he had got himself into, and by the fact that he was still digging. He had found it impossible to admit to Mel, in the conversation they had just had, that he had already had the required test. He should have come out with it then. But he couldn't. He had left it too late. If he did it now, he would seem mad. He would have to continue to live a lie, acting astonishment when the test results appeared, and never revealing to Mel that he had known the bad news all along. Feeling distanced from her by his dishonesty, he took her hand. He kissed it. 'I love you very much,' he said, his voice thick with suppressed tears. She put her head on his shoulder and made a happy noise.

~

The next morning Beale Pace woke up, gathered himself and listened. His house was silent. He sighed. They had all gone.

The birds had flown. This usually was the way of it, but it never failed to be disappointing.

Beale heaved himself out of bed. He looked down at his body, heavy, hairy and handsome, still slightly brown from the Ferrara holiday. Sitting on the edge of the bed, he watched to see if his abdomen creased into rolls. It didn't. It remained firm and, he thought, attractive. He took a few deep breaths, to see his belly muscles rise and sink. Then he got to his feet, and padded into the kitchen.

Harry's and Tally's cereal packets, spilt cereal, the burnt crusts of Sally's toast, milky bowls – why take so much more milk than you want? – spoons, knife, marmalade. He cleared the kitchen table in several journeys to the sink and the cupboards. He quickly rinsed the plates and cutlery up under the hot tap, deploring the waste of water, and wiped the table until it was perfectly clean. He set the chairs tidily, then got the broom and swept. This was his morning routine, sad and lonely. He put the kettle on to make more coffee; what was left in the cafetière looked murky. He went next door to turn on the TV, then returned to the kitchen. He danced around the room, humming and clicking his fingers, while the kettle finished boiling. His coffee was strong and black. He sat down in front of the news channel and, using the news as a background, tried to remember last night.

He had been watching the football, which he had settled to because Sally was working. Harry and Tally were watching it with him at first, but lost interest, and Harry went to his room, or to pester Sally, while Tally gave notice that she was going up the street to see John Greene. John Greene? Yes, you know, Dad, John Greene, he lives with his grandparents at Number Twenty-four. Beale remembered that part of the evening perfectly. Then Sally came out of her study with a happy cry of freedom and said she had finished work earlier than expected, and what about a drink together, and a nice chat, and the easy crossword. Beale was annoyed because he had become interested in the match, or wanted to say that he had. He started grumbling that everything was always on Sally's terms – he was watching football because she had insisted she had so much work to do, then she stopped working, and he was supposed to turn off the TV, just as the game was getting going. That started it. If he had accepted her overture as warmly as it had been offered, there would have been no row. And the irony was that he had wanted to. He would have loved to. He yearned to. He would have much preferred to be domestic and cosy with Sally for the rest of the evening than to watch the bloody match. He was punishing himself as much as her, and why? To make the point that he mattered. It was always the same. Coldly and haughtily she began the retreat to her study, and he pursued her, arguing. Most of the quarrel took place in her study. Drinking set in. He tried in vain to remember the rest.

As often, he now went into the spare room to look for evidence as to whether Sally had shunned the marital bed. The crucial thing always seemed to him to be whether they had ended up making love or not, and this was often difficult to remember. He looked at the duvet, which was straight, and the curtains, which were drawn open. He looked out of the window, and groaned. He hated himself and his life. He swore afresh never to touch alcohol again. Juan and Maria were passing the house at that moment and glanced in at the window. They began to roar with laughter together, he supposed at his nakedness, so he bowed and struck a few postures. They waved and he waved back. But hadn't he heard that Maria was very ill? Now his eye was caught by the corner of a piece of paper sticking out of the drawer of the bedside table. He opened the drawer and possessed himself of the paper. It took him a few minutes to work out what it was, then some more moments to believe what he saw.

It was a bank statement, but it did not apply to the only account Beale knew about, which was his and Sally's joint one. He saw immediately that it had £5000 in it. Then he saw that the account was in the name of S.A.B. Pace. S.A.B. meant Sally Antonia Blake, and that meant Sally. He stared at the paper, trying to make sense of it. He looked at the date. He was breathing hard and his mind was racing. Then he arrived at the only possibility that fitted the facts. Sally was secretly saving up to leave him, and had opened a personal bank account that would pave her way to a single life. To a life without him. Sweat broke out all over Beale. He would get her back. He would be so nice. He would not blame her for her treachery to him, the evidence of which was in his hand. He would be understanding of it. He would try to be grown-up. Please, please, please, Sally, don't leave me. Come back to me. You know I can't live without you.

~

Tally Pace was now a frequent visitor to John. She loved his attic. She brought birdseed. They stood on the desk with their heads out of the skylight and threw handfuls of golden grain on to the flat roof for the pigeons. Tally had named some of them, and John felt stupid because he could never tell them apart, except for the pale brown ones, which were his favourites, but even then he could not differentiate one from another. The first time Tally saw Benn, who was licking a hind leg on John's bed at the time, 'Lucky!' she cried, and sat down to stroke him. 'You've got everything,' she said to John. 'An attic. Pigeons and a cat. Lucky! What is his name?'

'Ben,' said John, having quietly cleared his throat. He did

not feel lucky, because of his impending death. He loved Tally coming, but he was still shy.

'He looks like the cat that used to live opposite us, only the old lady died,' said Tally, stroking.

'He is that one,' said John. 'Granny and Grandpa took him.'

'Unfair! Why not us? He lived nearer us.'

Anne fostered the friendship between John and Tally, and was always willing to include Tally at tea-time. So now she climbed the stairs to the landing and called up the ladder, 'Tea's ready!' and Tally hurried down, while John closed the skylight.

'Scones! Scones as well as cake!' Tally was saying to Anne. 'John is so lucky. I wish I lived here.'

Anne was pleased with what Tally had said. She wished John had been in the room to hear. Now Eric came into the kitchen. 'You here again!' he said to Tally. 'Good.' He turned to John, who was just arriving. '*Bonjour*,' he said. He tried to talk French to John sometimes, to help him with his worst school subject. Tally did not do French yet, but all the same managed to answer more readily than John did.

'Bon après-midi, you mean,' she said.

'I don't think they say that. You have to wait till it's *bonsoir*,' said Eric.

'You'd better ring your mum,' Anne said to Tally.

'She won't be in,' said Tally, busy with her phone. 'Dad might be.'

John and Tally sat down and Anne served helpings of tuna pasta with peas. Then she turned to Eric. 'Good news,' she said. 'Maria is all right. It wasn't cancer of the larynx. It was a benign lump and they've taken it out. She's home.'

'Good news indeed,' mumbled Eric, eating a scone.

'So if your voice goes funny,' said John, 'it doesn't have to be cancer?'

Tally looked up, noticing but not understanding an unusual intensity.

'No, it doesn't,' said Anne. 'People often get things in their throats. Also, the feeling of a lump can happen to someone who is trying not to cry.' A lump suddenly came to her own throat as she thought how often this had been John's experience, and that when she had been aware of these moments, how little she had been able to do for him. She added, 'It's a common expression, a lump in your throat. Here's jam and honey, in case anyone wants them with the scones.'

John ducked back into his pasta. 'Under the wide and starry sky,' he was thinking. 'Under the wide and starry sky.' It seemed they would not have to dig the grave and let him lie, just yet. His whole body seemed to swell and flush with joy. He concealed the joy, as fiercely as he concealed his tears; but he could not help a smile of delight overflowing in the direction of Tally, who, watching him, laughed a little.

~

Georgia was attempting a portrait of Anne. She had always enjoyed drawing and painting, ever since the crush on the art teacher, and the skill, or gift, had come in handy with regard to snails. She had not used it very much otherwise, or not in recent years. She had some unsatisfactory sketches of Brenda at the back of a cupboard. But Brenda had been a difficult subject, for she never remembered to keep still. Nevertheless, Georgia had been proud enough of those efforts to pull them out to show Anne, and Anne had been most gratifyingly impressed. So Georgia took her equipment to the Darwins every few evenings, and did her best. Anne was flattered to find herself sitting for Georgia. For both women, a respectable excuse to meet regularly and often was welcome.

79

Georgia phoned Anne. ' Hullo, Anne, it's me. Can I come over tonight for a sitting?'

'Yes. Do. Come early and eat with us. We've got a lot of tuna pasta.'

'Lovely. About seven?'

'About seven.'

Both went back more cheerfully than before to doing what they were doing. In Georgia's case it was looking out of the window at the couple opposite. The long-haired girl had the window open and was smoking. The short-haired man was coming and going in the background. Sometimes the girl looked inwards to speak to him, or answer him. Then she looked out again, and knocked ash off her cigarette. She did everything slowly. She never looked across the street. If she had, she might have caught sight of Georgia, and Georgia would have waved. Georgia did not believe that they took any interest in the street. This could be because they were leaving at Christmas. It was no good putting down roots. It could be because they were wrapped up in each other. Somehow Georgia did not think they were. There was a hint of boredom in the girl's posture, and she seemed to turn her head to offer a remark without enthusiasm. His movements were always brisk, as if resenting her leisureliness, and offering her a good example. Not knowing their names, Georgia called them Roland and Beatrice. Beatrice tended to wear dark clothes, usually sleeveless, and had elegant, slow-moving arms. Once, to her excitement, Georgia had seen Roland and Beatrice coming out of their front door, and had been dashed to perceive that Beatrice was wearing a very short skirt with black tights over plump thighs. Now Roland sat down opposite Beatrice in the window. He was eating. Georgia would have preferred it if he had brought a plate of food for them to share. But perhaps he had been offering to, and she had been turning him down.

She might be on a diet. Possibly that was why she thought it was a bad moment to give up smoking.

~

When Georgia arrived at the Darwins, John and Tally opened the door to her. They were laughing and excited about something. Tally was just about to go home. She stayed to greet Georgia, and then Georgia went unannounced into the Darwins' kitchen, where she had heard voices. Her eyes sought Anne, who turned from laying the table to smile at her.

'Ah,' said Eric. 'Georgia. What would you say to a glass of wine?'

'I'd say thanks but no thanks at the moment,' said Georgia.

'Steady hands for the great *oeuvre*?' said Eric.

Georgia did not have a reply to this, so she commented on Tally's presence in the house.

'Was she leaving?' asked Anne.

'Yes.'

'I'll just ring her parents to tell them,' said Anne.

'Surely she won't be kidnapped on her way up the street,' said Eric.

'All the same. Hullo, Beale? It's Anne Darwin. Just to say Tally's on her way home. Yes. Good. Okay then.' She rang off. 'So where's John? Did he go with Tally?'

'No,' said Georgia. 'He belted back upstairs.'

'Without saying hullo to you?' said Anne.

'Oh no, he did say hullo to me.' Georgia could not remember whether John had or not, but did not want this to be a matter for disapproval.

After the pasta and the remains of the cake, the three of them went into the sitting-room. Anne sat with her patchwork on her lap. Eric asked if they would mind a TV programme on certain buildings in ancient Rome, and of course they said they would not.

'Will we be allowed to talk?' asked Anne.

'Quietly. But you usually don't talk when Georgia's doing her stuff.'

It was true that they did not. Anne sat down, preparing to be as still as someone can be who is also supposed to be sewing. She took off her glasses. Georgia fetched the canvas from where it leaned against the wall, its front hidden from daily view, and stood it on her easel. She got her materials out and laid them ready.

Her idea had always been to have the patchwork in the picture. She wanted Anne to have a needle in her hand, but to be looking out, not down. Georgia did not require immobility, and Anne had got used to doing some unobtrusive stitches, tricky without her glasses, and then raising her eyes to Georgia.

Thus Georgia's large, rather watery, pale blue eyes and Anne's brown, small, shining, ones had frequent contact in the course of a sitting. Anne got over her embarrassment about this. For Georgia it was never anything but a pleasure. If their eyes met more than very briefly, looks of consciousness, recognition, affection and humour would come into both pairs. All this was part of what made the sitting such fun. These silent moments of intimacy were not reflected in conversation, or not yet, though their conversations, when alone together, were steadily becoming more personal and wide-ranging. Even so, Georgia had not seen fit to reveal that her only long relationship had been with a woman, and Anne had not mentioned the limitations she had always felt with Eric, though Georgia could suspect those for herself. Georgia child-sat occasionally, so they could talk about John, his reserve and probable unhappiness, and the fact that both of them had overheard him apparently reciting poetry to himself, which could not be normal for these days. Georgia spoke of the Tavistock, which

Anne had not even heard of, and instinctively recoiled from, but, as the suggestion came from Georgia, promised to think about.

Meanwhile the portrait was becoming rather good. It was certainly the best picture Georgia had ever painted. Georgia's idea had been that the figure should have patchwork lying on her lap and obviously be working on it; but that her face should show she had stopped for a minute, responding perhaps to a call of her name, or to a welcome person hoving into view. This had worked quite well, mainly because Georgia had managed to reproduce Anne's look of kindly curiosity, and had caught and even exaggerated the dark brightness of her eyes, usually, though not in the picture, bedimmed by glasses. There was no hurry to finish, and indeed for both painter and subject the longer it took the better. So Georgia could work slowly and laboriously on the detail. She always said the patchwork would take ages. Between sittings, when no one else was in the room, Anne would sometimes pick up the canvas and turn it round, and look with wonder at the careful paintwork and at her nice and interesting self.

Eric was surprised and admiring when he peered over Georgia's shoulder. 'Oh yes,' he said quietly, and had been heard to wonder aloud whether he should get out his own long disused paints, and have a go himself, after so long. It was Eric who showed the picture to John, who thought it was 'Brilliant'.

Chapter 8

Mel was at her parents' house for the evening. It was her father's sixtieth birthday, and a family get-together. Hugh had been supposed to go, of course, but he had made a lying excuse about an all-important work meeting. He telephoned Mel's mother and told her at length and in detail how essential it was that he should not miss that commitment. He found he could lie surprisingly fluently. He liked Mel's mother, and this made his mendacious rigmarole the more painful. Feeling as he did at the moment, and with the appointment for his test looming, he simply could not face Mel's family, her brother's little boy, her sister's baby; and he could not face seeing Mel longingly cuddling Tosie, while Mel's two siblings, perhaps, and their partners, looked askance at Hugh, or even made ribbing remarks, wondering why Mel was not yet a mother, when she was so obviously cut out for it. It had been difficult to square his ridiculous lie with Mel, and he had hated having to do it, but she had believed it.

~

Beale had decided not to tax Sally immediately with what he was calling in his mind her Escape Fund. That confrontation could not fail to escalate into booze and rowing. Experience, and perhaps an increase of wisdom through suffering, led him to this realisation. Instead, he had resolved to be incredibly nice. He would be so nice that very soon the thought of leaving him would become impossible, and one day he would see an unexplained extra £5000 in the shared bank account, about which he would say nothing, but merely rejoice in his heart. Some time in the future he might tell her that he had found out about her Escape Fund, and she would become aware of the mature and loving way in which he had managed that discovery.

He was angry with Sally at the moment, because she was to be at a meeting at work until all hours. He had succeeded in being incredibly nice when she broke the news of it to him last night. Now he was resentful. Tally was with John Greene at the Darwins; Harry had a football match. Beale had already been alone all day, a solitude broken only by a chat over the garden wall with Georgia, who had obviously been wanting to get back to whatever she was doing with her plants and snails. Other people had plenty to do; he had nothing. He had never been any good on his own, he thought. He blamed his mother. Other people of his age would soon be beginning to find their mums a burden and a liability, but not he. He would love to speak to his, but she was with a man he had never met and children he had not set eyes on, and lived in New Zealand, and his voice on the phone would surprise and possibly annoy her. He would be as unwelcome now as he had been when he was little. He thought what a good parent he was to Harry and Tally by contrast, and tears came to his eyes, unassuaged by the TV programme he was sitting in front of, which was about people having their homes embellished in their absence.

On the corner of the street there was a pub called the Viscount Palmerston. It was dark and cosy, dominated by a huge TV screen, but there was no football on at the moment, so the pub was quiet. Everyone in the street, and perhaps in other streets nearby, called it Pam's, which made newcomers to the neighbourhood think the landlady was called Pam, to which name she enjoyed answering, and she also liked her special link to the real denizens who knew her name was Cath. Thither at six o'clock, on that particular day, coincidentally, slunk both Hugh and Beale; Hugh on his way back from work and knowing there was no Mel at home; Beale desperate to get out of his empty house.

Beale and Hugh were no more than acquaintances. They were at different stages of life. Beale had his smart wife, youthful indeed but technically middle-aged; Hugh's wife was still very much a girl, a girl in jeans with long blonde hair. Beale had children of school age while Hugh's tormented thoughts about the next generation reached no further than a newborn baby, perhaps even no further than a pregnancy. Yet in age only four years divided them.

When Hugh came into the pub, Beale was at the bar, talking to Cath. There were solitary people, or people in pairs, at about half the tables. Early evening on a weekday was not usually busy. The sight of Beale's back at the bar made Hugh wish he had not come; he had hoped for a short, quiet and miserable pint entirely by himself. But Beale turned round and saw him, and with a 'Thanks, Cath,' approached Hugh's table.

'Can I buy you a drink?' said Beale. Hugh could hardly refuse. They drank, and the next thing Hugh knew he was buying Beale one, and they had got talking.

It was Beale who brought the conversation round to unhappiness, and specifically, the trials of marriage. Hugh had heard, as who in the street had not, that Beale and Sally had quarrels. He was intrigued to think he might now be told an inside story, an account of the relationship from a horse's mouth. He was enjoying the sense of instant friendship that was part of

Beale's demeanour, and, if you fell for it, part of his charm. Meanwhile Beale was asking Hugh questions, but Hugh did not want to answer, and said he was very lucky and he was very happy and his marriage to Mel had no problems. 'Ah, stonewalling, eh?' said Beale. 'Well, that's fine.' Thus it was, as the pints went down, that Hugh, whom Beale hardly knew, but now liked, was the first person to whom he confided his discovery of the Escape Fund.

'Don't tell anyone, not even Mel,' said Beale. 'This is top secret.'

'No, I won't tell anyone.'

Tears were in Beale's eyes now. 'You see why I am so frantic,' he said. 'I love Sally, I am mad about Sally, and now I know she's planning to get away from me, because I'm such a monster.'

'But are you such a monster?' asked Hugh, who could not imagine it. Beale appeared to him rather gentle and malleable. A bit silly, perhaps, but scarcely monstrous.

'We have these awful rows, and they're my fault. I start by complaining about some ridiculous thing, and they escalate.'

'Any chance she gives as good as she gets?'

Beale had self-pityingly hoped a thought like this might stir in Hugh. But he did not really believe it, and he did not take it up. He was silent for a moment. 'Anyway,' he said, 'what I've decided to do is be incredibly nice. The stakes are so high now that I must never quarrel with her again. I never thought I might drive her away from me. Never. And here she is, establishing an Escape Fund. From me. Who loves her more than anything on earth and more than any other man ever could.'

'Look,' said Hugh, wanting to be helpful. 'Let me think about this. Aren't you jumping to conclusions? You find that Sally has recently opened a new bank account in her name only. In it is five thousand pounds. That's all you know. The rest is conjecture. Stop there and think again. It does not have to be an Escape Fund. What else could it be?'

'You tell me. I can't think of anything else.'

'She could have come by a bit of money she wants to keep to herself for the moment. I don't know why. To give you a treat for your birthday? A surprise Christmas holiday for the family? If she's been saving up, putting money away, five thousand pounds seems a remarkably round sum for the fund to have arrived at.'

Beale had not thought of that. ' Yes, it does,' he said. 'Come by a bit of money? How?'

'Parents?'

'No, they are poor as church mice. He is a church mouse, actually – a retired vicar.'

'Bonus from work?'

'Hardly. She had one in June.' Hugh's train of thought, meant to be comforting, had disturbed Beale. The terrifying shadows of new possibilities were emerging in his mind. 'Do you mean,' he said. 'Do you think . . .'

Hugh began to realise what he had done. 'Look, you're probably right,' he said 'It's the Escape Fund. You're the one who knows her.'

Or did he? thought Beale. He put his head in his hands. Suppose the Escape Fund theory was a fantasy? He had thought of it as the worst imaginable scenario; but perhaps it had been a defence against something even worse. He groaned quietly and stood up. 'I must be getting home,' he said. 'It's seven. The kids will be back.'

'I'm sorry,' quavered poor Hugh. 'I seem to have said the wrong thing.'

'You've opened my eyes to other possibilities,' said Beale. 'That's all.' But in his heart Beale was cursing Hugh.

They walked silently along the street until they reached

Hugh's house. They said goodnight and Beale crossed to the opposite pavement and opened his front door.

Tally was furious. 'Dad, you made me come home at seven and you aren't even in. I could have stayed at John's.'

'Sorry, darling. I'm a bad dad. But it's only ten past.'

'Twelve. And where's Harry?'

'Football. They had a match.'

'Mum?'

'Meeting. Did Anne give you tea?'

'Yes.'

'Good.'

'And another thing, Dad. Fenella had to be late for school and she saw you sweeping, nude. Willie flapping, she said. Why can't our family behave normally?'

'Too late now, darling. I have my routines. I get up, I clear up the mess in the kitchen you two and Mum make with your breakfast, I shower, I get dressed. In that order.'

'Well, it's disgusting.'

Beale was trying Harry's phone. He really should be home by now. The phone was switched off. 'Has Harry phoned?' he asked Tally.

'I don't know, I haven't been in, he hasn't phoned my mobile.'

Beale checked the answerphone on the land line. Moments like this made him feel powerless. He went to the front window and looked out. 'If he's going to be late he should phone,' he said.

'No good being cross with me,' said Tally.

'I'm not cross.' Beale came back into the kitchen to start cooking something for Harry and himself. Sally had said not to bother for her. If I start doing something else, thought Beale, any minute I will hear Harry's key in the door.

He heard Harry's key in the door. 'Dad's cross with you,' said Tally.

'I'm not,' said Beale. 'I'm cooking bacon and eggs for you. How was the match?'

Harry told him.

The children dispersed, and Beale sat down to think. One thing he knew. When Sally got home he would ask her about the money. If it was not an Escape Fund, what was it? Conjecture was no good. Only Sally could tell him. And, he now thought, what if she was not at a work meeting? What if her doings this evening were part of a double life, as was the money?

～

Sally really was at a long, tedious and important meeting, and she came home exhausted. Beale was waiting for her.

'What's the matter?' Sally asked, seeing Beale's face.

'I have to tell you,' said Beale. 'Last week I found a bank statement. The account was in your name only. To the tune of five thousand pounds.'

'Oh God,' said Sally. 'Yes.'

'Explain.'

Luckily for Sally she was angry with Ron. She felt he had ignored her during the meeting, and any special relationship she had with him seemed to have been forgotten or erased. She told Beale about the cheque from him.

'I didn't know what to do with it,' she said. 'It seemed a pity to waste it. At first I wanted to tear it up, then I thought we could use it. I couldn't put it into our bank account, or you would have noticed. So I opened another, just for it.'

'But why did he give you the cheque?'

'He thought I'd done a lot of extra work, and he thought he could get it back off expenses.'

None of this was too bad, if true. 'Are you sure you aren't carrying on with Ron?'

'Very sure.'

'Okay. Now, what we are going to do is this. You write a cheque for five thousand from the new bank account into our bank account. First thing tomorrow. Make sure I get up before you go to work. Then, tomorrow, close the new account. I will write a cheque to Ron Basquette for five thousand pounds. I shall do it now. The cheque will come to him in my name, not yours, though it's from our joint account. I'll post it. I want him to know you told me about this and I'm involved. There'll be no more cheques from him.'

'So we can't keep the money?'

'No.' Beale was feeling happy. 'I've been imagining awful things. What I've got now is peace of mind. For the first time since I saw the bank statement.'

'Where was it? I couldn't remember where I put it.'

'You hid it in the drawer in the spare room bedside table.'

'Oh yes. Beale, I must say, you are being incredibly nice about this.'

'Oh,' said Beale, 'but I am incredibly nice. Now, you're dead tired, it's late, get to bed and to sleep before I start making love to you.'

'Or after,' said Sally.

~

Hugh would have been tempted to break his word to Beale and tell Mel all about the interesting conversation in the pub, except that he had to keep up the pretence of the meeting at work. Mel arrived home full of her own family and of how much Hugh had been missed. She had a slightly squashed piece of birthday cake for him. Hugh fetched a plate and a fork and ate it then and there. After all that beer he had forgotten about supper, and was hungry.

They were both aware that in his lunch-hour the next day Hugh was to go the clinic in Harley Street where he was booked for his test. He was in suspense. His hope was that his sperm would have improved with the passage of years and under the influence of love. But perhaps it would not have.

'Will they tell me at once?' he asked Mel. 'Or will I have to wait for results?'

Mel didn't know.

'I'll have to wank,' he said gloomily.

'It's only the once,' said Mel, who had also realised this, and did not like it either.

'What if I've forgotten how to?'

'Make sure you think of me.'

Hugh did not say, 'They'll give me magazines of nude models,' for this might have shown too much knowledge.

They went to bed. It was not policy to have sex the night before the test.

Mel went happily to sleep. She did not expect bad news. Hugh could not sleep, lying on his back, staring into darkness. The likelihood was that the test would produce the same profile as last time. Conceivable that it would not; probable that it would. He did not know how Mel would take it. It would not be easy for her. There was much that was as yet unknowable about what would be unleashed when he broke the news. But that was not the very worst thing. The very worst thing was that he had been dishonest to Mel, and was continuing to be so, and could see no way out of it, ever. Tomorrow he would have to pretend to Mel that he was as shocked and astonished by the result as no doubt she would be. He could not tell Mel the truth. For two years, or for however long within that time she had been worried about her fertility, he had allowed her to go on worrying. That was the inexcusable thing. He had known about her fears, and had known how depressing and how omnipresent they were. He

93

knew that with the passage of time they had inexorably become worse. He had said nothing. If he had told her the truth, she would still have been worried, but about a deficit in him. As it was, he had cruelly allowed her to go on assuming that the deficit was hers. Why had he done it? He was afraid of how the information would affect her feelings for him. She might stop loving him. He delved a little deeper. She might stop admiring him. He might have to do without her idealisation of his masculinity. In the darkness of the night he detected in himself another version of the phallic swagger which had got him into this mess in the first place, had got him into this mess the day he agreed to bestow sperm on Min and Terry. He cried a little, and put his face against Mel's smooth shoulder, careful not to disturb her. In order to sleep at all, he made himself imagine that he would come through the test with flying colours. 'Yes, perfectly normal,' the medical voice said in his mind. 'Would you like to have a look down the microscope yourself?' And there were his spermatazoa, crowding the drops of seminal fluid like so many shoals of fish and overwhelming each other with their motility. 'Wow!' said the white-coated man. Hugh slept.

Chapter 9

Anne, Georgia and Sally stood in a group outside Anne's front gate. Anne had been outside, her arms crossed, her cardigan tightly doubled against her thin chest, looking up and down the street; and first Georgia, then Sally too had stopped. It was what Eric disparagingly called a Mothers' Meeting.

Anne had important news. 'Number One has been bought.' For months Number One had been in the process of being done up. First there was scaffolding, then cleaning, scraping and painting, with a band of men in and out of it all day, and machines whirring and humming. Everyone thought it looked beautiful, and it occurred to more than one street-dweller that it might be time to have their own outside painted. Then it was For Sale, and potential buyers could be seen viewing it. The residents of the street who were interested in such things watched the viewers closely, wondering who were the ones destined to become their neighbours. 'I don't know who the buyer is,' Anne said, 'but I have it on good authority from the house agent that it's definite.' Anne knew all the house agents.

'How exciting,' said Sally. 'Newcomers.'

'What sort of people would you like it to be?' Georgia asked, addressing the question to both.

'A retired couple would be rather nice,' said Anne. 'Nice for me and Eric. Perhaps a bit boring.'

'I'd like famous people,' said Sally. 'What about Timothy West and Prunella Scales? They might help Beale with his career. The house has been made quite posh enough now for famous people to want to downsize into it.'

'What about a community of four nuns?' suggested Georgia. 'That would make a change. There must be four bedrooms.'

They got involved in working out the likely number and positioning of the bedrooms, which was less interesting, though interesting for Anne, as a property surveyor. While this was the topic, all three spotted Maria coming along the pavement in their direction. Maria stopped. Sally was the only one who had not seen Maria since her reprieve, and it was an opportunity to hug and rejoice. Then Anne said to Maria, 'You'll be getting new neighbours. Only two doors away from you.'

Surprisingly, Maria knew all about it. 'I have met him,' she said.

'Met him? Met the buyer? Have you?' the others chorused.

'Yes. He is very nice.'

'Just one person?'

'Yes. An old man. On his own.'

This created a little disappointment.

'Was he friendly?' asked Anne.

'Yes. He did a magic trick for the children with a five pence piece. I hope the children do not disturb him.'

'You've got Number Three in between,' said Georgia.

'Yes, but I mean in the garden. In the summer.' Maria was a known worrier.

'What is his name?' Anne asked.

'I don't know. He said it but I have forgotten.'

'An Englishman?' asked Sally.

'Yes. What I call very English.' Maria laughed, but now moved on, heading for the shops. She was still treading on air.

She was going to live. Everything and everyone in the street was bathed in a blessed ordinariness.

The other women watched Maria out of sight. They too were smiling. After their brief reverie on life and death, Anne sighed and said, 'What you expect to see moving into the street is a young couple, say Mel and Hugh, or a young couple with one child, say the Hodgkins at Number Ten, or else couples retiring. Or a single busy career person, like Georgia. That's the size these houses are.'

The others concurred. 'Yes,' said Sally. 'We aren't moving, but it's a squash for us.'

'It's a squash for Juan and Maria too,' said Anne. 'They haven't got so much built on at the back as you have.'

'Tally's room is tiny,' said Sally. 'Above the porch. Where lots of you have bathrooms. The trouble is we do really need a spare bedroom.' She did not say why.

'I'm so glad John and Tally get on so well,' said Anne.

This might have been a moment for Sally to thank Anne for having Tally to tea, but she was never home from work early enough to witness this innovation, and it was not the kind of thing Beale told her. So she merely said, 'I am, too. Tally loves your cat.'

'It's Brenda's cat,' said Georgia. 'I agree with Anne. You don't really expect a person who buys a house in the street to be a lonely old man.'

There was a short silence while all three digested this description. They all knew he might not be lonely. But until they learned his name, he was to be referred to by these three and by some of the people of the street they talked to as the LOM.

∼

As far as Mel knew she expected a text saying 'Everything fine'. So she was not on tenterhooks as the time of Hugh's appointment came and passed. At two o'clock she got a text saying 'Bad news. Could be worse. Tell you later.'

'Bad news. Could be worse.' From her internet researches Mel knew exactly what this was likely to mean. Hugh was sub-fertile, but not infertile. She struggled with the idea, which she now felt had been expected as well as unexpected. She could not concentrate on work. She asked her nice female boss if she could go home, and told her why. Talking about it, she cried. The boss spoke of the joys of IVF, which was just what Mel did not want to hear. But she was allowed to leave early.

At home, she stood looking out of the window with a cup of tea in her hands exactly as she had stood a few weeks ago when so jubilant. The jubilant feeling was still there, if she reached for it, but it was now diluted with other feelings. One was sorrow, a sneaking, private sorrow for her body, which was perfect, but its perfection wasted. It might as well not be perfect. It made her think of a wonderful plant blossoming in a place where no one was ever going to see it. She felt disappointed in Hugh, even annoyed. Then she felt guilty for those feelings, and concentrated on being sad for him. He must be crestfallen indeed, and her first thought must be to make it all right for him. They had both been so certain that if there was something amiss it was in her. He had sometimes pretended otherwise, but neither of them had believed it. What a blow for him. Then she was conscious of a tiny bit of mean triumph. He had always been so cocksure about himself. Live and learn, Hugh, live and learn.

She was on the computer looking at IVF sites when Hugh came in. She switched off and hurried to the door. They hugged. Then each thought about what had happened, and hugged for longer. Hugh took off his rucksack and they sat down.

'No tea,' said Hugh. 'Just stay with me.' He held her hands.

Her face asked him to tell her how it had gone, and to take her through every moment. He began. He had waited, then he had been called, then he had been asked questions by a very gentle man who looked Indian, or possibly Bangladeshi. Questions about sex, as you'd suppose. Then he was directed to a booth where there were nudie mags. He didn't look at them. There was a container to wank into, and eventually he managed. Then the wank was collected by a brisk nurse and he was sent back to the waiting-room. At last he was called, and this time there were two men in the consulting room, the Indian, and an Australian. The Australian was a doctor. He explained that Hugh's sample showed that he had fewer sperm than average and that they were less mobile than average (Hugh could not embark on 'motility', though that term had resurfaced). Hugh was sub-fertile. However, he was not infertile. At any time pregnancy could occur. It was just that the chances were were not so high as average. They were only twenty per cent. That hadn't sounded too bad, to Hugh, twenty per cent; and it did not sound too bad to Mel. Hugh did not tell Mel that the doctor had suggested he come back to be retested monthly for three months. He had refused that offer. Then the doctor tried to issue him with a special condom that collected sperm during intercourse, and, when brought to the clinic the next morning, might possibly provide a higher reading. Hugh rejected this, and omitted it from his account for Mel. He left, having paid even more than he had foreseen.

'I'm so, so sorry,' he said, after a short pause, meaning more than Mel knew. 'So, so sorry.'

At his words, she was immediately and fully sympathetic. She put her arms round him. 'Don't be,' she said. 'It's not your fault!'

They were hugging again, perched on their uncomfortable kitchen chairs. 'Are you going to leave me?' he said.

'Yes,' said Mel. 'I'm going to go off with Beale Pace.' It was known that Mel could not stand Beale.

Mel made more tea, and they talked. They discussed IVF, which Hugh had never deigned to do before. Mel was careful not to show herself in too much of a hurry to get started. They talked about maleness, and what a crushing blow this was for Hugh. He said he did not want his humiliation to overwhelm all other feelings, especially his empathy with Mel, about how much she must be going through. He said she was being very brave. They had a word or two about how each was likely to feel about sex in the aftershock of this event. He said it was the most awful thing that had ever happened to him. Mel tried to cheer him up. She did not say it was the most awful thing that had ever happened to her, though, actually, it was.

'If you'd known about this,' he said, 'when we were first together, would you have wanted to stay with me? To marry me?'

Mel was silenced, for she could not answer this. It was too difficult. She could not let him hear that she would have reluctantly left him. But that was probably the truth. So she said, 'Don't let's talk about troubles that didn't happen. We've got enough troubles without that!'

Hugh was surprised at how easy it was to behave, and, more, to think, as someone who had not foreknown the bad news. He understood that this was because when he had first heard it, six years before, he had not taken it in, or not taken it in as he did now. He had briefly been upset, but he had shrugged it off, and managed not to experience the meaning of it. He had not allowed it to change or chasten him. So there was a sense in which he, as much as Mel, was now learning it for the first time.

It was painful for Hugh that Mel did not know the whole

truth, but all the same he was feeling better. He had not been completely honest, but he felt as if he had. Or he felt as if he had been more honest than before, honest enough to look Mel properly in the eye. This made him very happy, a private happiness tucked away behind his unhappiness for her and his concern for their future.

~

'I've got to talk to you,' said Tally to Harry. He was headed for homework, but stopped when he heard her urgent whisper. 'I need to tell you a secret. We've decided to let you in on it.'

'What?' he said.

'There's something awful going on at Number Twenty-Three.'

'You mean here in the street?'

Tally nodded, as if gestures were safer than speech. Then she lowered her voice still further. 'They've got a prisoner,' she said.

'How do you know?'

'You can see from John's skylight. You can look into their top window.' She gestured to bring his ear closer to her mouth. 'She's being kept prisoner.'

'No need to spit. How do you know?' But he was interested in spite of himself.

'We're keeping notes. We decided to tell you. You can come over and look tomorrow after school.'

'Okay.'

So the next day Anne had Harry as well as Tally to tea, and left a telephone message for Beale to say so. The cauliflower cheese that was supposed to do for grown-ups' supper as well as children's would have to be augmented. Georgia was coming. Anne considered options. She had plenty of home-made dishes in the freezer.

Three heads could not fit in the skylight at the same time, so Tally encouraged John and Harry to have first go. She stood on the floor very close to the desk and listened to what they were saying.

'D'you see her?' said John. He was whispering, although no one but Tally could possibly overhear.

'Yes. But she's just sitting on a bed. She doesn't look . . .'

'She's beginning to stand up. Watch. We think they beat her up.' The nameless girl got laboriously to her feet and reached for a stick. She crossed the room to her desk and sat down. 'You see? She can hardly walk.'

'Let me see, let me see,' said Tally, and John jumped off the desk to give way to her.

'You see she's reaching out,' said Tally. 'That's for the telephone. Look, she's trying to make a phone call.'

'Maybe she's just phoning,' said Harry.

The door of her room opened, and she immediately put down the phone. 'See?' said Tally. 'That always happens. She doesn't want her captors to know she's trying to make contact with the outside world.'

The person who had come into the room was a young man with a tray. 'See?' said Tally. 'That's her iron rations.'

The young man put the tray down on the desk. If the two spoke, it was very cursorily. 'Now he'll go out again,' said Tally. 'Locking the door behind him, we think.'

But he did not go out immediately. He moved to the windows and drew the curtains.

'He's drawn the curtains, John,' said Tally, speaking downwards.

'They do that,' said John, speaking upwards to Harry. 'It's all part of the captivity.'

Harry and Tally jumped down. The three of them sat on the futon where Benn was already ensconced. Tally stroked Benn as they talked. She fondled his ears. He began to purr.

'What's the evidence that she's a prisoner?' asked Harry sensibly.

'One,' said John, 'she is always in that room. Always. Two, she limps, like someone who has been hurt. Maybe when she tried to escape. Three, we never ever see her out of doors, and we've seen the two men from the house out in the street and we recognise them now. They don't look wicked, but you can't go by that. We call them C1 and C2.'

'What's C for?'

'Criminal. We call her V.'

'V for what?'

'Victim. Four,' said Tally, 'They never speak to her for long. Five, no one but them ever goes in her room. Ever. Six, we have seen her crying. She tries to stop when one of them comes in. That's pride, probably.' Tally had her notebook out now. 'Seven, she sometimes wants to open a window, fiddles with a lock, can't open it. They must have made it too stiff. They wouldn't want us to be able to wave to her.'

'Do they know about you?' said Harry sharply, anxious.

'We don't think so. We always make out we're feeding the pigeons if one of them looks our way.'

'We've got to be careful,' said Harry. 'Smile if you see them in the street. Don't look at them suspiciously. They might get scared and retaliate.'

'Okay,' said John.

Tally was making notes, to keep her entries up to date. She balanced her notebook on Benn.

Anne, slightly out of breath, could be heard calling them down for tea. John and Tally were both happy that Harry was in the secret. 'It's not iron rations here, I can tell you,' muttered Tally to Harry as they all jumped downstairs.

～

Georgia was looking at Anne over the remains of the cauliflower cheese and a dish of thawed home-made meatballs with the

103

sort of look that Eric noted and marvelled at. 'I just think you're wonderful,' said Georgia.

'Why?' asked Anne, who had never in her life seen herself in that light.

'Having the Pace children to tea all the time. You are so generous. So flexible. So unselfish.'

'It's not all the time, and today was the first for Harry.' Anne did not advert to it, but her life was enriched beyond words by Georgia being her friend. It showed even in her body. She had put on a little weight, and lost a few wrinkles.

'The first of many, I predict. And the food you cook is always so delicious. These meatballs.'

'Have some more.'

Georgia did. 'Any news of the LOM?' she asked.

'Not yet,' said Anne.

'The LOM,' said Eric. 'That's what you call the man who has bought Number One. Yes. I meant to tell you. I have news of him. Amazing news. I know exactly who he is.'

Anne and Georgia were all ears.

Eric spoke to Georgia. 'I had a heart operation twenty years ago.' Then he spoke to both women. 'I saw Mr Packington, the heart surgeon, outside Number One! Of course he's much older. Even then he must have been in his sixties. So he'd be eighty-odd now. But it was him all right. I don't forget a face. I didn't like to say how-do-you-do to him, because he would never have recognised me, and because he was feeling for a key in his pocket and looking rather frail. He had a young woman with him. Well, when I say young, Georgia's sort of age. Then he found the key and they went into Number One.'

Anne was more interested than Georgia, because, of course, she remembered Mr Packington very well, and, in his time, which fortunately for Eric had been fairly brief, he had been a household word. It took Anne a while to stop exclaiming.

She said she wished Eric had spoken to him. An argument threatened to begin, behind which was the weight of Anne and Eric's differences about whether to foster community in the street. Georgia intervened with a question to Eric about how and when glass was first invented. Peace returned.

Chapter 10

Laurence Packington was phoning his sister. 'Isabel, I've been trying to get you.'

'Well, here I am.' Isabel's voice was frosty.

'I'm sorry I can't be more help,' said Laurence, picking up the frostiness, and making a vague effort to thaw it. 'Has he moved in?'

'He's moving in this week.'

'He could afford live-in help.'

'Of course he could afford live-in help. He refuses to have it.'

There was a silence, then Laurence said, 'How is he?'

'Well, you know how it goes.'

'Will he be all right, on his own?'

'I doubt it.'

'Oh God, Isa.'

Isa had thawed. 'I wish you were here, Larry.'

'So do I. What can I do?'

'Nothing, I suppose.'

'Perhaps we shouldn't have let him buy this house.'

'We couldn't stop him.'

Another silence. Then Laurence said, 'Funny he was perfectly all right until Mum died.'

Isabel didn't pursue this. They had pursued it often. Instead, she said, 'In a way he's done something very sensible, completely normal, selling the family house, downsizing, and ending up with somewhere nice to live and lots of additional income.'

'Yes, in a way it's perfectly normal.'

'What I hate is I always think you want me to move in with him. Which I can't do. I've got my life.'

'I know.'

'I'll go and see him, obviously. I'll phone him every day, as I have been. But live with him I won't. Why should I? Just to give you peace of mind?' Isabel had moved from frosty to heated.

'Of course not. Will you let me know how the move goes?'

'Yes. Phone me on Thursday evening.'

'Friday morning for me. I'll phone you before work.'

They rang off, Laurence troubled, Isabel resentful. A lot of their phone conversations ended like this.

~

Few people in the street were unaware of the arrival of a huge removal van at Number One.

'The LOM is really called Mr Packington and he's a heart surgeon,' Tally told her parents.

'Who's the LOM?' asked Harry.

'Mr Packington,' said Tally.

'Mr Packington,' repeated Sally and Beale, trying it out, getting used to the idea.

'Is he that really old geezer,' asked Harry, 'white hair and a stick?'

'I don't know,' said Tally. 'I haven't seen him. I only know who he is.'

'Philosophical,' said Beale. He went to the window to look out. 'There's a big removal van,' he said.

'Who doesn't know that? It's been there for ages,' said Tally.

~

Next door, Georgia was looking out of her window. She could see the removal van if she looked up the street. But her eyes were more attracted to the house opposite. Beatrice was sitting at the open window, cigarette in hand. That was a frequent sight. But it was days since Georgia had seen Roland. Had he left Beatrice? Was he on a holiday? Was he away for work? Georgia tried to deduce from Beatrice's demeanour whether she had been abandoned. Beatrice smoked and sat, as ever. It was a Saturday, so Beatrice would not be going to work. She was in no hurry. She seemed at peace. Was she pleased to be rid of Roland? Had she thrown him out? It was hard to imagine Beatrice doing anything as dynamic as that. But you never know.

There was a ring at Georgia's door bell. It was Sally Pace.

'Come in,' said Georgia.

'I just wanted to tell you the LOM's arriving,' said Sally.

'I've seen the van.'

'He's really a heart surgeon called Packington.'

'I know. Coffee?'

Sally sat down, and, making coffee, Georgia said, 'He did Eric's heart.'

'Is that how we know who he is?'

'Yes.'

Sally glanced at the paper until Georgia brought cups of coffee and sat down. 'I never have time to read the paper at home,' she said.

'Well,' said Georgia, 'you're so busy.' Georgia was thinking how elegant Sally looked, even on a Saturday.

'I have to be,' said Sally, 'as the only earner.'

Recognising the dig at Beale, and determined to preserve her neutrality, Georgia said nothing.

'Now,' said Sally, 'I want to ask you something. I've realised the kids are usually at Anne's after school until nearly eight o'clock. They're often still there when I get in from work. I feel guilty. Beale does nothing about it of course. Anne feeds them. What can I give her as a thank you? And what on earth do they do there? You must know the grandson.'

Georgia concealed her intense pleasure at being regarded as an insider to Anne's life. 'John. He's quiet. Clever. Sweet.'

'Has he got computer games they play? Do they play in the garden? What do they do?'

'They have a game in the attic. I don't know what it is. You're not worried, are you?'

'Not a bit. I just want to be kept in the picture. I'd better go and see Anne. But what shall I take? Flowers? Champagne? Chocolates? She's been feeding Tally for the past month and now she's started feeding Harry as well.'

'Anne's like that,' said Georgia.

'I know you're very close to her,' Sally said.

It drifted into Georgia's mind to say, 'I'm in love with her,' startling Sally as much as Sally's utterances sometimes startled her. She did not say it. She said, 'Perhaps one of those big beautiful strings of onions you hang up in the kitchen.'

~

'The LOM's furniture has arrived,' said Hugh to Mel, as he came into the house from buying the paper. Mel moved to the window to have a look. Number Nine, which was their house, was not that far from Number One, with odd numbers only in between.

'Oh yes,' said Mel, interested, looking at the removal van. 'Do you think that's a daughter? Perhaps the OM is not all that L.'

Hugh came to look over Mel's shoulder. A brisk sixtyish woman was standing on the pavement, directing the removal men. Her loud, middle-class voice could be distantly heard. 'Very likely a daughter,' agreed Hugh. He put his arms round Mel's waist from behind and joined his fingers tight. 'Will we have a daughter who looks like that in sixty-five years?' he said. He would not have been able to make a joke like this before the recent troubles. Now he could, and Mel could giggle. Nor could he have risked the parody of possessiveness that his joined fingers suggested. It had surprised them both that something light-hearted which had not been there before had surfaced in their relationship. Sex itself was more light-hearted. Hugh did not feel he must offer himself to Mel as a stud, and she did not fret about whether she was giving satisfaction. They could be fallible, and even, at times, ridiculous. Contrary to expectations, they were having as much sex as they had ever had, but it was not solemn. It did not have to be significant. Neither of them was polishing a performance. As a result they were closer. Emotional formalities they had not known were there had been effortlessly dropped. Hugh was not trying so hard to be manly; Mel could walk naked in front of him without worrying about whether or not she looked beautiful. She still had her disappointment and he still had his guilty secret, but neither pain was as heavy and implacable as it had been before. Tackling the pregnancy issue had been postponed until the new year, still nearly three months away.

~

The removal men had driven away, and Max Packington and his daughter Isabel sat in Number One. They were in the downstairs room, which went through the house from front to back. They were both sitting on armchairs, but permanent places for furniture had of course not yet been arrived at. Boxes surrounded them. A sofa stood tall on its arm. A television, plugged in and ready to go, perched on an upended desk.

This was an occasion when a chicken casserole from Anne would have been welcome, and indeed it had crossed Anne's mind, but she had decided it was premature. Isabel had foraged in the high street for a takeaway. She and Max ate pizza out of its cardboard box. Max did not eat very much.

'Before I go,' said Isabel, ' I must find the things you will need to make coffee in the morning. I will leave them laid out in the kitchen. The kitchen is at the back, next to the garden. Everything works. It's a lovely house, Dad, you have done well.'

'I don't believe I chose it,' said Max. 'But I'm glad you like it. It can be yours after I am dead.'

'I bought two croissants while I was out,' said Isabel. 'I'll put them in the kitchen with the coffee materials. You will eat them for your breakfast.' She disappeared for a few minutes, and when she returned, she said, 'All in order. It's your same old kettle, so perfectly easy to turn on. I've left a glass of sherry there too, in case you want it later.'

'How very nice. You have thought of everything, darling.'

'I'm so glad there are fitted carpets everywhere, and a perfectly acceptable colour. There are two telephones, one in here, next to where you are sitting now —' Isabel gestured, to make sure Max saw it, 'and one upstairs by your bed. I have made your bed, though there's chaos all around it. And on the box by the bed is the second phone. Of course you've also got your mobile.'

'Where is it?'

'In the top pocket of your jacket.'

Max's hand groped. He took his mobile out of the pocket and looked at it.

'I shouldn't take it out unless you want to use it,' said Isabel. 'Or you might mislay it.'

'But I might want to use it now,' answered Max thoughtfully. 'To ring who?'

'You. Or perhaps Laurence.' However, Max sensed that his suggestion was not going down well, and put the mobile back in his pocket.

'I've done a nice big notice of phone numbers,' said Isabel. 'Here it is. I don't quite know where to pin it. What would be the most convenient place? There's my phone number, and my mobile. Then there's Dr. March. Then there's 999. Then there's your own new phone number here. We can add to it, as things crop up. Shall I pin it on the inside of this door? Then you will see it whenever you are in this room.'

'I daresay all the numbers are in my address book.'

'They are. But when people have moved house they can't always lay hands on their address book when they want to.'

'Can I see the notice?' Max studied it for what seemed to Isabel an excessive amount of time. She rattled four drawing pins in her hand and waited. Then he said, 'I wonder where I have put my reading glasses.'

'Jacket pocket,' said Isabel, rattling. 'Right-hand lower pocket.'

Max found them and put them on. He looked at the notice again. 'Ah yes,' he said. He did not want to part with the notice, but Isabel could not relinquish the idea of pinning it up. He watched her.

'I know you think I am dotty,' he said, affectionately. 'But I know my name is Max Packington, I know you are my daughter Isabel, I know I have moved house to Number One Palmerston Street, I know my wife died, I know I am a cardiologist, I know I am eighty, eighty something – well, what would it be? I know I was born in 1926.'

'You are eighty-six, Dad, and very good for your age.' Isabel had been heartened by her father's last utterance. All this was hard for her. She had adored him. She had lost the person she had adored.

'Do you think there's a lavatory here?' he asked.

'Yes. I've shown you. A small one on this floor. The bathroom upstairs.'

'Ah-ha.'

'Shall I show you again?'

'No. I'll find it.'

'Well, Dad, I'd better be going. I'll pop in tomorrow, after work. Phone me if there's anything.'

'Yes, I will. Thank you, darling.'

'Your radio's on the box beside you.'

'Ah-ha.'

'Would you like the TV on?'

'Yes, why not? Thank you.'

'News channel?'

'Yes.'

Isabel adjusted it, and pitched it rather loud.

'The remote is just the same as it was at home,' she said, putting it in his hand. 'Is that all right?' She slipped out of the room and the front door, unable to face the spectacle of Max puzzling over this familiar object.

～

Max watched the news. When he got tired of it he stood up and went to look at Isabel's notice, pinned to the door. He took it down, and went back to his armchair, the better to study it. He was still wearing his reading glasses, which he was glad of now, and that explained why the TV pictures had been obscure. He looked at the telephone numbers written on the notice. It all made perfect sense.

Then he remembered Isabel had said something about sherry. He successfully located the kitchen, and the shelf on which she had arranged instant coffee, sugar, a small milk carton, the kettle, two croissants, and a glass with a reasonable amount of sherry in it. He returned to his chair, carefully carrying the glass. He sipped, contentedly, and looked again at the TV.

Now he wondered what time it was. The TV announced it. Sixteen minutes past nine. He could go to bed soon. Tomorrow would be another day. He did not seem to have a clock. He had got out of the habit of a wrist-watch in all the years when constant scrubbing up had made a watch an inconvenience. Perhaps Isabel knew where one of the clocks was. He picked up the telephone, and looked closely at the hand-written notice. He presumed she would have designated herself 'Home', and rang that number. It was engaged. He rang it several times. Then he spotted a number named 'Isabel', and dialled that. She answered at once.

'Dad. How are you doing?'

'I can't find a clock.'

'A clock. Oh golly. I forgot. I don't know. I'll find one tomorrow.'

'What time is it?'

'Twenty to ten. You could go to bed.'

'I'll need to know the time in the night.'

'Keep the radio on.'

Max realised there was nothing Isabel could do before tomorrow. 'All right. Good night, darling.'

He took his stick and went to the front door. He opened it and looked out. He waited. After a few minutes a young couple approached from the left. 'Excuse me,' said Max, 'I wonder if you could tell me the time?'

Hugh and Mel stopped. 'We know you have moved in today,' said Mel. 'Welcome.' They introduced themselves.

'We live at Number Nine,' said Hugh. 'If there's anything we can do.' He tilted his watch towards a shaft from the street light, and said, 'Five to ten.'

'Thank you.' Max went indoors again, careful to close the front door. Five to ten. He would go upstairs and to bed. He squeezed his radio into his jacket pocket and, pleased by the young couple, heartened by the sherry, triumphant at finding the lavatory, he prepared himself for the first night in his new house.

Chapter 11

Beale woke, listened to his house, and found himself, as usual, alone. The sun was streaming through the curtains, and he registered that it was going to be another bright October day. Brightness did not agree with Beale. It brought home to him, more than dullness did, that others might feel cheerful, that the day was long and that he would be on his own.

He groaned quietly and got up. A lot of people, he thought, would give their teeth to be able to go swimming this morning, on what they would be calling a lovely day. He had the opportunity to go swimming, but he could not make himself want to. Might an early swim motivate him for the day? Perhaps it would. But he could not motivate himself for a swim, and that had to happen first.

He cleared up the breakfast and made coffee. He took the cafetière into the sitting-room and sprawled in front of the TV news.

What he needed was a job. He should give up on the hope of acting and even of its demeaning derivatives. He should hawk himself up and down the high street. It would be a cash-in-hand job, probably, if he succeeded in getting one, and would not swell the bank account; but he could use the cash to buy food, so the bank account would be less pressured. It would come to the same thing. Would Sally be more pleased or more humiliated?

He wasn't sure. Suppose Eric Darwin said to her, 'I saw Beale stacking shelves in Tesco,' it might be humiliating, but if Eric said, 'I saw Beale helping clear the grounds at the derelict church,' she might be impressed. He had to think of the children, too. He did not want Harry saying, 'Jimmy says his dad is your boss in Sainsbury's, and you are really slow,' or Tally saying, 'You'll have to get dressed in the morning, won't you, now that you've stopped being middle class.' But whatever anyone thought or said, the time had come when he had to do something.

He thought a haircut might help, so as soon as he had showered and dressed he headed for the high street, and the cheapest barber shop.

'Do you know of any jobs?' he asked the barber, as he sat in front of the mirror, and reflected on how his face was ageing. Perhaps that was drink. No, it was the passage of time. Or both.

'Jobs?' said the barber. 'Do you mean hens' teeth?'

Beale sighed. It was as he thought.

'Nice head of hair, still,' said the barber.

Beale wanted to say, 'I'm only thirty-six,' but held his tongue, in case the barber thought he was lying. He paid and left. He walked up and down the high street for half an hour, regretting his haircut whenever he saw himself in a shop window, and afraid of Sally's reaction to it. There were no advertisements of vacancies. However, the morning had passed reasonably painlessly, and he popped into Pam's on the way home. Surely the price of one beer could not break the bank.

Cath liked Beale, and found him attractive. She was pleased to see him. 'Your hair!' she said.

'Horrible, isn't it,' said Beale, as his hand went to his unfamiliar head, as if to cover it from view.

'No, I like it,' said Cath. 'Half of bitter?'

'Yes please. You haven't got a job for me, have you?'

Cath had seen Beale twice on TV, and needed some convincing that his question was serious. 'I know,' said Beale. 'You are thinking how I have come down in the world. Well, I have.'

But surprisingly, Cath was interested in his query. She said it might be useful to have Beale to fall back on. They had mild ribaldry about that. Sometimes, she said, she was more busy than she expected. How would it be if she gave him a call when she could do with an extra hand, and if he was free he would come in? For Beale it was better than nothing. He agreed. She gave him an hour's training there and then on the few people who wandered into Pam's at lunch-time. Beale had no difficulties.

It was not a job, but it was something. Beale went home feeling encouraged. He was not sure how work in Pam's would go down with his family. Better than Tesco's, anyway. And perhaps the fact that it was casual made it more acceptable. It was evident to him that Cath would not mind an affair with him. She was blonde, forty and divorced, and although he was not particularly attracted to her, he was energised by the notion that she fancied him. The brightness of the day was now more in keeping with his mood. However, he had been faithful to Sally, and intended to remain so.

~

Tally was well into her second exercise book. The doings of the people opposite were being carefully catalogued. Tally left the exercise books with John, for what Harry called security. John stowed them between *Mr Midshipman Hornblower* and *A Ship of the Line*, always in the same place. But sometimes when the others were not there he would take them out and read them.

Their covers were both inscribed; 'ABSOLUTELY SECRET. OPEN AT YOUR PERIL. John Greene, Heironimo Pace, Tallulah Pace, Ben Darwin.' The entries were always dated and usually quite brief. 'C2 brings tray to V. Puts it on table. Talk for a minute. Goes out shutting or locking door.' Reading them was always fascinating for John. He read and re-read them, loving Tally.

Harry had introduced binoculars. He was the one who used the binoculars most. Tally couldn't fix them to suit her eyes. They were too big for her face. John became scared of seeing the amount of detail the binoculars showed him. One evening he had seen a shining tear on Victim's cheek, blushed, and quickly passed the binoculars back to Harry.

Neither Harry nor John knew whether they believed in the story or not. Tally did believe it. But to both John and Harry it was such a good game that they could not relinquish it. They believed it and didn't believe it. They did not let on to each other or to Tally that, actually, though a wonderful story, they knew it was a tall one. Tally was the one who advocated telling the grown-ups and going to the police. The boys, fearing the end of the game, said that shouldn't happen yet because evidence was still being gathered. So Tally filled her exercise books.

There was discussion at the moment about whether a message could be sent to V by a pigeon. The pigeons had become very tame, and it might be possible to attach a message to a leg. This had not yet been tried, and the pigeons tended to shift away if anyone tried to touch them. But even if the message could be attached, how would the pigeon be trained to stand on V's windowsill with it, and knock with its beak?

One evening Tally decided to disobey the boys and tell Beale. Harry was at football.

'Dad,' said Tally.

'Yes.'

'Something really funny is happening at Number Twenty-three.'

'Who lives there?'

'Three French people who call themselves students.' And so the story came out. 'You do believe me, don't you, Dad?'

'I absolutely believe you think what you are saying is true. But all the same it might not be. The facts you've described could have other interpretations. We'll have to find out.'

'How?'

'I'm going to ring on the door of Number Twenty-three. Coming?' So they went together, Tally awed by the ordinariness of the plan, and alarmed at what Harry might say. It didn't matter about John, because he always liked whatever she did.

'What are you going to say, though?'

'That I've heard they're French, and that I wonder if they might offer French conversation classes.'

'But that's mad!'

'It doesn't matter. Just to talk to them.' But no one answered the door.

'You see? They're pretending to be out,' said Tally. 'She's up there, all alone.'

'Plan B,' said Beale. 'Anne. She's sure to know about them.' They crossed the street and rang Anne's doorbell. Anne asked them in.

'No, we won't come in,' said Beale. 'Just to ask you a question. Do you know anything about the French students opposite?'

Anne did. Indeed earlier in the day she had taken them a chicken casserole. There was a brother and sister, and there was a friend. They were all from Lille. But the sad thing was the sister had MS, and in the last month had come down with a bad attack. The brother thought the parents should come over and fetch her home. They might be going to, quite soon.

It was too much responsibility for the young men to look after her. The brother, who was the one Anne knew best, was called Jean-Luc.

'Have you actually seen the sister,' asked Tally, 'with your own eyes?'

'Yes, I popped up today to her room, right at the top of the house, which I think is stupid. She should be on the ground floor. She's very depressed. Marie-Christine. Only twenty. She came over to study, and now she can hardly move. But you do have remissions, with MS. And attacks can be psychological. I think she'd be better at home, and I've said so.'

Beale thanked Anne and quickly turned to go, fending off her likely curiosity about why he had wanted to know. Tally walked beside him, crestfallen and pensive. So the game ended. The boys were less astonished than Tally had feared, when she revealed the truth to them. She continued to visit Anne's, though less often; there was still the attic, the skylight, the pigeons, the cat, Anne's delicious teas, and John. Harry returned to his previous pursuits. The binoculars were left in John's room, and John managed to teach Tally to use them. Together they studied pigeons, cracks in chimneys, the texture of roofs, and the ever-changing sky. John was pleased that Tally did not want her exercise books. 'Chuck them!' was her instruction, but John did not. Beale said nothing to anybody of what had happened, in case the children were made to feel silly. He did not even tell Sally, who was liable at times to find telling a funny story irresistible.

~

'Are you happy with Eric?' Georgia asked Anne.

'Of course I am,' Anne answered. 'Whatever would be the point of not being?'

The humour of this reply dawned on both of them, Georgia

first, Anne after half a minute. They chuckled. Their relationship had reached the level where questions such as this one
were fairly commonplace. For Anne, it was a hitherto unplumbed
depth, and the humour was new too, and she was enjoying it,
though it made her feel guilty and raffish.

Eric was at Pam's, intrigued in spite of himself at the notion
of Beale behind the bar. Anne and Georgia had the patchwork
and the paints out. Tally had gone home, John was upstairs.

'I'm glad Tally came this evening,' said Anne. 'She's not
come so often recently. John might miss her.' Anne said this
partly because it was on her mind; partly to stem the intimacy
stirred by Georgia's question.

'Why is she coming less often, do you know?' Georgia asked,
busy with her palette and brushes.

'No. And we haven't seen Harry for days, not that he was
ever a frequent visitor like Tally.'

'These things happen, I suppose. Relationships fluctuate.'
She sat back to look at Anne, who did what she could with
her needle and the patchwork, for the sake of the portrait, but
found it difficult without her glasses. Georgia watched her
fondly. 'I'm glad ours hasn't,' she said.

'Ours?' Then Anne understood, and answered seriously. 'Yes,
I am too, very glad.' Again she felt the urge to lower the
temperature, and said, 'How is the picture tonight?'

'As excellent as its subject is wonderful,' said Georgia.

'Silly girl,' tutted Anne, looking down and smiling into her
lap.

The picture was coming on. The loose coloured squares,
and the cascade of finished quilt, still had a long way to go; but
the central figure, thin, steadily sitting, looking out at the world,
eyes friendly and speculative, hands at work, was a joy to see.

Anne had never in her life before been an object of interest,
and she was thriving on it. She had been busy, generous, sociable,

skilled, efficient, necessary, a family member, she had been a lot of things; but she had never gained, nor dared to seek, attention. This did not mean she had not been important to people. She had been. But nobody's mind had dwelt on her, or speculated affectionately about her, or quelled a racing heart at the sight of her, or had her in dreams. She had not seen excitement, excitement about herself, in the eyes of anyone looking at her, nor had she ever known a glance her way turn into a gaze. She had not consciously missed these things. How could she miss them? She had a plain, busy mother who did not look at her. She married a man who did not look at her, either because she did not know how to be looked at, or by chance. Thus what she saw in Georgia's eyes when she met them with her own was new to her. So was the obvious fact that Georgia found it hard to take her eyes off her. One of the meanings of the portrait was that it was an excuse for Georgia to look at her freely and intently without arousing comment. Comment was aroused, however. Eric had referred to Georgia as Anne's 'fan', and Sally Pace had made the observation that the two were 'very close'. At nearly seventy, Anne was learning a lesson proper to youth and its first bloom: how to be an object, as well as a subject. It was wonderful. Sometimes it was too rich. There were the moments when she looked and smiled back into Georgia's eyes, open, tremulous, whole-hearted; then there were the moments when she wanted to run away and make a macaroni cheese.

She had always liked and admired Georgia. She had admired Georgia's independence, and the fact that she had not succumbed to marriage. Since she had known Georgia better, she had admired her enterprise, her scholarship, her artistic talent. She was impressed to think of Georgia in the Sinai desert, studying snails, and camping under the stars to find out what the desert species does at night. She liked Georgia's thick, shoulder-length hair, blonde and grey, and the way

Georgia would run a hand through it. She liked Georgia's voice. She liked the sturdiness of her body, in comfortable skirts and flat shoes. The scene was set for love, but love was not alive and active in Anne until Georgia fell in love with her. Then it was, and her main feelings about the Sinai expedition now were that its two-month length would be painful, and that Georgia must come safely home. She did not know, of course, that Georgia had curtailed her trip because she could not face being so long away from Anne.

Eric came back from the pub. He stood behind Georgia, looking at the picture, his breath beery over her shoulder. 'Well,' he said, 'Well.' He paused to choose his words. 'If I was a youngster I would say wow.'

'That's high praise,' said Georgia, putting down her brush, feeling the time had come to bring the sitting to an end. 'How was Beale in the pub?'

'As to the manner born, I'd say.'

'He's acting a barman,' said Georgia, 'I suppose. It's the actor in him.'

'He's cut his hair.'

'Does he give change right, and all that sort of thing?' Anne wanted to know.

'As far as I could see. Cath is lovey-dovey with him.'

'Oh dear.'

'Probably only acting, for Beale,' said Georgia. 'I don't think Sally has much to worry about there.'

'Let's hope they're too sensible to have an affair that would impinge on the street,' said Anne. 'That would cause ructions.'

'The street, the street, the street,' said Eric, accusing Anne.

'Well, it's important,' said Georgia, not for a minute recruited to Eric, which he had hoped she would be.

~

Max Packington's house was becoming habitable. Isabel had men round, and the furniture found places. The house still did not have a lived-in look, for the pictures were stacked against the walls; there were still unopened boxes; the bookshelves were empty of books. Isabel promised herself she would do all this gradually. The important thing was that Max was comfortable, and had a chance of beginning to feel at home. He knew where things were in the kitchen. Deliveries of food were organised. There were curtains in the sitting-room and Max's bedroom, and there would be more curtains when Isabel got round to it.

'Perhaps I'll come over after Christmas,' said Laurence on the telephone, 'only for a short visit, I'm afraid.'

'Good,' said Isabel.

'How is he?'

'He's weathered the move remarkably well, I think. And the neighbours are very nice. There's a woman called Anne, the other end of the street, who brought him some soup, and says he fixed her husband's heart twenty years ago.'

'Was he pleased? To be reminded of work?'

'Yes. And pleased the chap's heart is still going strong. But he's not forgotten work. That's a thing he hasn't forgotten. A whole lot of DVDs about the heart fell out of a box when I was unpacking, and he watches them all the time.'

'That's a good sign.'

'Yes. He says the heart is still not understood. He says it's so wonderful. All that sort of thing. He'd happily give anyone a lecture. A young woman was with him when I arrived the other evening, and he was explaining the heart to her, watching a DVD. She is a few doors down. Mel, I think.'

'You might say he's fallen on his feet.'

Isabel did not want her brother too carefree. 'Well,' she said, 'he has good moments.'

'And the bad ones?'

'He loses everything. A list of phone numbers I wrote out for him and pinned up. He unpinned it and lost it. He loses the phones and the remote for the TV. Often when I arrive he is looking for something, or asking me to.'

'And does it turn up?'

'Yes. You have to know where to look. There was a telephone in the fridge, and the watch I got him, because he fusses a lot about the time, was strapped to the handle of his walking stick.'

They both laughed a little, against their better judgement, and Laurence said, 'But he never wears a watch.'

'No, but I thought he might start now, as he says he can never see a clock, though I got two big wall ones, one for downstairs, one for upstairs. Another nice neighbour, Juan, saw me through the window trying to put them up and he came and helped, did it in seconds. Dad tried to inveigle him into the heart DVD, but he didn't have time.'

'It all sounds quite friendly.'

Again, Isabel feared Laurence's mind was too much at rest. 'He's very frail, of course,' she said.

'Does he go out?'

'Yes. Up and down the street, at least. And there's a pub at the end. I think he goes in there. I haven't mentioned to anyone that he's forgetful, because I don't think that would be fair. If they find out, they find out.'

'Which I fear they will.'

~

Meanwhile Max sat quietly on the chair which seemed to have been designated as his. He was watching a DVD of a heart operation, not one of his own. 'You chump,' he said aloud. 'If you leave that where it is it'll cause trouble sometime. Ease it out now! Oh, you chump.' Max watched closely. The DVD came to an end. Max did not succeed in starting a new one.

Max had a notebook, and now he took it out of his pocket. Somewhere in it were instructions about the DVD machine. He turned the pages. Phone numbers. Three for Isabel, home, work and mobile, written by her in big, dark numbers. Then there was something about the microwave. But where were his glasses? They were not in his pocket. Perhaps he should make an appointment with the optician. But he could not find the optician's number in the notebook. Then he had forgotten that he was looking for the optician's number and he had forgotten that he was looking for the DVD instructions. He was puzzling, instead, about who Dr March could possibly be. 'March,' he muttered, as if the sound of the word might awaken the memory. It rang no bells at all. So he closed the notebook, and slowly stood up, wondering what time it was.

The struggle to stand up reminded him that he was old. He had a train of thought he quite often had, though he did not remember it between times, so it always felt new. When would he die? He did not forget – he never forgot – that he was old. He suspected it was high time to die. What was going to give out? His heart, probably. The heart is a wonderful organ, but it does not go on for ever. Or it could just as well be a stroke. So he pondered, standing up, his legs staggering slightly.

The phone rang. He located it and picked it up. It was Isabel.

'Good news, Dad,' she said. 'I've sorted out the cleaner problem. Mrs Gray is coming.'

'Mrs Gray?'

'Yes. The cleaner you had in Muswell Hill all those years. Josie Gray. It's further for her, but she's prepared to come, for you.'

'Josie Gray.' Max did not want to reveal to Isabel that so far as he knew he had never heard of her.

'Yes. She's coming tomorrow morning. You'll have to be in, but then we can give her a key. I'm so glad. It'll be continuity for you.'

'Continuity,' affirmed Max. But how could there be continuity if his memory had gone? 'Thank you, darling.'

Chapter 12

Sally's life had taken a turn for the worse. Her normal time for getting home from work was half past seven or eight, usually nearer eight. Until recently, Beale would be longing to see her and would dance attendance, hoping she had not brought work home. Now, not always, but on an awful lot of evenings, Beale would greet her briskly with, 'Glad you're back, I'm due at Pam's at eight.' He would have prepared some supper for her which she would eat alone, slowly and gloomily, doing the easy crossword. The children were usually in, and soon she would have to start suggesting that it was bed time. In the past Beale had usually done all that, on the understanding that she was tired after her day. Or they had done it together, which could be fun. Nowadays, the children in bed, she went to her study to work, or, if she did not need to, attempted to devise a reasonable pastime for herself until, at about half past eleven, Beale reappeared.

Now Sally regretted the pressure she had put on Beale to earn money. Her salary was adequate for the family's requirements, and her expressed wish for Beale to contribute had the character of a card in her hand in quarrels, a piece of self-righteousness for her to fall back on, rather than of a genuine cry of need. She was paying for it now, she thought.

She couldn't walk down the street without meeting at least

one person who wanted to talk about it. Once it was, 'Beale makes a good barman, hidden talents,' from Eric Darwin. 'We saw Beale working in Pam's last night,' said Hugh Davis. 'It must be nice for you that Beale is bringing in a bit of money at last,' was Anne's reaction. Sally thought she should forestall these irritating conversations by calling out, 'Beale is working in Pam's, I do know,' but she was too polite.

She knew Cath fancied Beale. On the rare occasions when Sally and Beale had had a drink in the pub, this had been obvious to Sally, though Beale claimed he had not noticed it. He had, of course. He could not fail to see the caressing looks and smiles Cath turned on him, while ignoring Sally almost to the point of rudeness. Was this why Cath had given him the job? And did Beale know this was why Cath had given him the job? Sally did not suspect an actual affair. For one thing, at least so far, opportunity must be lacking. And Cath was not in any serious way Beale's type. But what Sally hated to imagine was a scene of jostling closeness, giggles and vulgar *doubles entendres* behind the bar from Cath, and a look of curbed response and regretful marital fidelity on the face of Beale. And half the street would know! It would be an interesting pantomime for all the neighbours, and one in which Sally felt she was utterly humiliated.

Sally had not been able to talk to Beale about it, beyond asking, 'You're not carrying on with that brassy blonde in the pub, by any chance, are you?' which query did not do justice to her more complex fears, and, of course, was an idea Beale repudiated. Asking the question, even jokingly, as she did, lowered her status in her own eyes, and evoked from Beale raucous crowing that she was jealous.

Sally was not used to entertaining herself, nor good at it; and now felt she had not been sympathetic with Beale for those long evenings when she brought work home. Although the children were twelve and ten, it was not her and Beale's practice to leave them alone in the house at night. Tally was liable to nightmares, and Harry might sneak out of bed to play on the computer. So Sally stayed in. She talked on the phone with friends, read the paper, tidied a cupboard or two, kept the children up to watch TV with her. Once or twice she tried to get Georgia to pop over from next door, but Georgia was out, probably up the road with Anne. It was loneliness that made Sally begin to obsess about Beale and Cath. She found herself keeping track of sex, in fear that Beale was less horny with her due to getting it elsewhere. This was not proving to be the case, but she had never before felt a need to keep tabs on sex in that way, and it grated on her. She sometimes felt an unfamiliar dislike for Beale, wondering whether he was meanly punishing her for making him jealous of her relationship with Ron, and for leaving him too much alone. If this was retribution, it was exact, and it was working very well. So Sally looked at Beale with new ambivalence, which she was fair-minded enough to try to disguise, recognising that his motives might be blameless. An advantage of their new pattern of life was that both she and Beale were drinking less. Sally never had a desire to drink alone, and Beale arrived home more or less sober. They had a whisky together when he came in, which was all that seemed to be left of their old convivial life. Another benefit was that they were not quarrelling. This was partly because they had less time together in which to work up into a row, but also that Sally's confidence was dented, and Beale was not so thin-skinned.

Sally had never worried about the fact that she was ten years older than Beale. Why should she? She was remarkably young-looking for her age and he not particularly for his. She was not the sort of older wife who has the unpleasant experience of being taken for her husband's mother. This had never happened. Most people didn't even know, and if told, they were astonished. Did the street know? She was not sure. But now it did come into Sally's mind; not in relation to Cath, who must be well into her forties herself. Sally bought expensive rejuvenating face-creams off beauty sites on the web, in a way she had not before.

She began to long to see Beale and Cath together. What she yearned for was relief – the sight of a busy pub, or a quiet one, and the two bar people each doing what needed to be done in a different part of it, perhaps shining up glasses, or having a word with a customer at a table. That would set her heart at rest. She began planning. She could drop in at the pub for a drink. Why shouldn't she? The fact that she had never done so before did not mean she never could. She might make an appearance, casual and elegant, with a light laugh and a look of mischief, slim where Cath was fat, and ask Beale or Cath for a gin and tonic. Why not? The trouble was that Beale would know immediately that it was a subterfuge and a ruse, and she did not want that. He would also know, or suspect, that she had uncharacteristically left the children alone. Perhaps she could pretend she had enlisted Georgia. That would be an outright lie. But she would leave the children asleep, she need only be gone twenty minutes, and surely nothing would happen to them in that time.

She had no alternative but to spy. Outrageous though this notion was, she could not get it out of her mind once she had conceived it. As far as she could remember, Pam's had various windows, and these she could peer through without being visible from within. Or so she hoped.

It was half past nine and the children slept peacefully. Sally changed into jeans and a hoodie and slipped into the street, closing the front door quietly behind her. She still did not believe she was going to do it. She believed she was going to walk round the block and come home. And yet, physically, she was keyed up as if she was going to do it. The night was not cold, but dark, and drizzling rain was falling which Sally had not expected.

She arrived at Pam's and walked on as if she was going to pass it by. Then she stopped, for she had spotted a small window at her eye height. It was irresistible. She looked around, and saw no one on the pavement. The street seemed to be empty. Boldly she stepped up to the window and looked in. At first she could only see the back of someone sitting at a table. As her eyes accustomed themselves to the odd perspective, she saw more. She saw Beale standing behind the bar, idle but ready to serve, and her heart lifted with love. She could not see Cath. Then it occurred to her for the first time that perhaps Cath sometimes summoned Beale so that she could have the evening off. Perhaps she and Beale were not necessarily on duty together every time. Sally had not thought of this before.

To her annoyance the door of the pub opened and someone came out into the rain. Instead of moving off at once, he stood and looked about him. Sally was annoyed. He had had plenty of time to put up a brolly, if that was what he was fidgeting about. No brolly appeared. He was standing and looking around, and now began grunting quietly to himself. Sally did not want to look straight at him, in case they recognised each other, and there was embarrassment. Whatever would she say she was doing? Her behaviour was just as odd as his. She turned her back on him, although by doing this she lost her viewpoint through the little window. She waited impatiently. But now she heard a voice.

'Excuse me,' it said. 'I wonder if I could trouble you. I live at Number One Palmerston Street. I have lost my bearings. Which way should I go?'

Sally thought quickly and understood that she was having a rather unorthodox introduction to the LOM, *aka* Mr

Packington. For the moment, politeness overcame all other feelings, and she turned to him with a smile. 'Yes, of course,' she said. 'I'll walk you there. It's not far. My name is Sally Pace. We live at Number Eighteen, on the other side of the street from you.'

He thanked her and they began to walk, he leaning on a stick. Sally now realised that he *was* old. She took sideways glances at him, glances illuminated by street lamps, in whose light the spears of drizzle gleamed. His handsome face was lean and craggy, and his thin hair white. She had set off at her normal walk, but now slowed down, in case she was making him hurry. 'I'm most grateful,' he said, several times, and Sally answered as she should. She was dawdling now, afraid she had heard him breathing heavily. They arrived outside Number One. She waited while he groped for a key, he thanked her again, and they said goodnight.

Freed, Sally headed back to the pub, almost at a run. But as she passed her own house, on the other side of the street, with its lighted windows, she slowed down. She became undecided. Somehow the urgency had gone out of the spying. She had seen Beale, and she had not seen Cath. It was partly that. There was an urge to have another peer, but it was much less strong. And the children were alone. She knew it was irrational to be relieved by not having seen Cath. Cath might have been no more than temporarily out of eye-range. Another peer might reveal her. Irrational or not, Sally did not want to tamper with her unexpected feeling of peace, of which increased trust in Beale was mysteriously a component. Also, the encounter with Mr Packington seemed to have reduced Sally's level of anxiety. It had been an interesting meeting, and she had been able to help. She liked him. How strange that he did not know the way home. And what must it be like, thought Sally, to be so old, so frail, alone in a dark street?

So Sally let herself into her quiet, brightly lit house, in which no activity from the children was evident. She took off her damp clothes and put them in the wash, as if to expunge her excursion into spying. She had a bath and washed her hair and put on her pretty dressing-gown. She wanted to be composed and ravishing when Beale arrived.

Beale always found her ravishing, and particularly liked that silky garment, through which you could tantalisingly see the details of Sally's shape. He took her in his arms. He was no more than mildly beery. 'Kids okay?' he said. 'I've missed you. How has your evening been? Work?'

'Just ordinary,' she said. 'Nothing much. All news is with you.'

'It is, actually,' said Beale, beginning to organise whisky. 'A little bit of news. Mr Packington came into Pam's. The LOM from Number One.' Sally showed interest, and Beale went on, 'He ordered a dry sherry and a packet of crisps. He forgot all about the crisps – here they are, no point wasting them, have one – and after a while had a second sherry. He stayed for about half an hour. We chatted.'

'Is he nice?'

'Very. A lovely old boy.'

'What did you talk about?'

'The heart, a bit. He was a heart surgeon. Then other things, how he feels about moving into the street. That didn't work very well, because he said he lives in Muswell Hill. He's a bit confused. Then as he really does seem pretty old I risked asking him if he was in the war.'

'Why "risked"?'

'Well, he could have said, Excuse me, laddie, I was only ten when the war ended.'

'That would have been awful.'

'Luckily it didn't happen. In fact he was in the Arnhem landings in 1944. But he didn't want to talk about it. Feeling silly, I said I had seen *A Bridge Too Far*. It took him a while to understand that it was a film, and he obviously hadn't seen it. Then he gave a grim guffaw and said, "A bridge considerably too far, I'd say." He asked if he could buy me a drink. Of course I refused. You must meet him.'

Sally liked hearing Beale talk about the pub in a way that showed interests so different from the ones she had been surmising. She felt abashed and happy. Certain that Mr Packington would not recognise her, she said she would love to meet him, and Beale went on, 'We've got a few old boys on their own, regulars, who sit at different tables and have a few drinks. They sit in the shadows. Talking to them, you see their memories are shaky. I think they prefer to think they're fuddled in a pleasant familiar way, a way they're used to, by alcohol, than to feel fuddled in a horrible new way they can't understand. By age, Alzheimer's. Sometimes they have a bit too much. But they obviously get home all right, because they are there the next evening, at their table.'

'And did Mr Packington leave all right?' asked Sally innocently.

'Yes. He's got a walking stick, he uses that.'

'I don't know why we have to call it Alzheimer's all the time these days, even when people are very old,' said Sally. 'What's happened to gaga? Gaga is much nicer.'

'Yes, much nicer. Whatever we call it, it'll come to us all, if we're spared long enough. Have you finished your drink? Let's get to bed. I've been wanting to ever since I got in. If not before.'

~

Mel had put pregnancy from her mind, and was not going to think about it until after her thirtieth birthday, which was two months away in December. She had not been at all sure that she would be able to relinquish the preoccupation, and had expected it to seethe privately, concealed from Hugh, who was resigned to the fact that the subject would re-emerge as an IVF project after her birthday, or, as he put it, fighting for time, in the new year. With so much settled, Mel had found she was able to take a holiday from her hopes and fears. She had put on a little weight, becomingly, and was quite enjoying work. She didn't worry about subtracting alcohol from her diet or adding folic acid to it. All that could wait. Meanwhile she was happier and, consequently, so was Hugh.

And yet as soon as she was two days late with a period, she knew it immediately and, immediately, the feelings that were in storage unrolled and unpacked within her and were everywhere again. She hoped, she feared, her heart pounded with alternating bliss and anguish, she waited in suspense until the moment came to buy a pregnancy test. She did not know when that moment might be, and was afraid it would be soon; and whenever it arrived the wonderful hope that, willy nilly, had invaded her heart would be lost. So she managed not to buy one on the way home from work, and then it was too late and the chemist was shut and Hugh had come home. So five days had passed before she bought the fateful oblong box which she knew so well and so bitterly. In all that time she had succeeded in not telling Hugh.

Often in the past she had not told Hugh. She bought test kits from different chemists, so that the assistants at the local one would not pity her. 'That poor woman.' 'That poor woman was in again today.' 'Shame.' She must have done the test at least ten times, she thought. Hugh had known about a few of the tests, and, indeed, had assisted at the first two, holding the all-knowing stick in the stream of her urine. This time, he was not going to know. He was only going to know that the test had happened if a purple line appeared in the 'test' window, matching the purple line in the 'control' window. She was sure this wouldn't happen. Why should it? It never had before.

She went into the bathroom with the kit while Hugh was cooking beef stew and dumplings. The delicious smell penetrated the whole house. Her hands were trembling, her breath was quick, but she carried out the test steadily. She stood up from the loo, laid the stick on the handbasin without looking at it, and stared out of the window. 'Please, please, please,' she was saying under her breath. She needed a bit of time to pass, to conform to the instructions. 'Please, please, please.' It was exactly like all the other occasions when she had done the test. It was exactly like all the other occasions, except that when she turned and picked up the stick, there were two purple lines on it, not one.

She felt like giving an ear-splitting scream of joy, but instead, she checked carefully that there was no mistake. It was some time since she had last done a test – had she misremembered? She had not. But she made sure. She even fished the instructions out of the packet, with that familiar tiny print, and reread them, although she knew them so well. She closed an eye, in case stress had given her double vision. Certain, she walked demurely out of the bathroom and into the kitchen. She was holding the stick between a finger of her right hand and a finger of her left.

'Turn round,' she said to Hugh's back. 'I don't want to drop this into the beef stew.'

He turned, looked, understood, put down the wooden spoon, took the stick from her and held it to the light. She watched his face. Then he laid the stick on the table and folded her in his arms. First they jogged a bit, then there were a few dance steps.

'That's okay then,' said Hugh. 'You clever, clever girl. You beat the twenty per cent.'

'No, you did.'

'I did nothing,' he said. 'I can't believe it was so –' He hesitated, looking for a word, then laughed and said, 'So easy. After all that, it was so easy.'

~

Roland was back. Georgia stood in her sitting-room with her hands round a cup of coffee and watched the window opposite. She was glad Roland was back. Why had he been away? For the first time, his mother's funeral occurred to Georgia. She dismissed it on the grounds that if that had been happening Beatrice would have been away too. Not certainly, however. Perhaps Roland's family disapproved of Beatrice. Or perhaps she hated them. Or perhaps Roland and Beatrice could not afford two fares there and back to Zimbabwe. Or Colorado. Or Sydney. Whatever the explanation, he was back. Georgia looked at him closely, suddenly caught by the possibility that it was not Roland. Roland had never had as distinctive an appearance as had Beatrice, and one young man in a black tee-shirt and jeans was, to Georgia, much like another. But his demeanour was Roland's. He was brisk. Now he was on the telephone. Indeed they both were. As far as Georgia could judge, Beatrice did not look like a person who had taken up with a new lover. Now she was opening the window, her phone in her other hand. She sat on the windowsill as so often, but, what with the window and the phone, did not have a spare hand for a cigarette. Or perhaps she had given up smoking, in honour of Roland's return. She finished her phone call, and Georgia saw the phone pushed into a trouser pocket. Then Beatrice looked out over the street. She was contemplating the view. That was unusual, but it was an irresistibly bright and crisp October morning, with the smell of autumn leaves in the air, and, though it was chilly, it was not unpleasantly so. Georgia's hand came to shoulder-level, ready to wave. Beatrice's wandering gaze was arrested. She had seen Georgia. Georgia waved. Beatrice waited a moment, then waved back. It was a puzzled, awkward wave, but it was a wave.

'Beatrice waved to me this morning,' Georgia told Anne later.

'How nice,' said Anne. 'At last. Did Roland?'

'Roland was unaware, I think.'

'Are you going to call, now she has seen you? Ring their doorbell?'

'No, I don't think so. It's nice as it is. Relationships shouldn't always have to be pushed further.'

Anne was not so sure, but went on cooking. A few nights ago, after the sitting, Georgia had taken one of Anne's hands and pressed it to her lips. That had pushed the relationship further, at least to Anne, and wonderful it had been. Georgia was thinking about that moment as well.

Chapter 13

'Mr Packington was in the war,' Tally told John.
'Fought in the Second World War?' exclaimed John.
'Yes.'

'How do you know?'

'Dad said.'

'Do you think he'd let me interview him?'

'Well, I don't know but you could try.'

'I've done my five questions, but I didn't think I'd ever
find anyone.'

'Okay, well, you have.'

'They have to be really old.'

'Not as old as the ones in the First World War. But I
think they are all dead.'

'Will you come with me?'

'Yes. But we haven't fed the pigeons.'

'We can do that later, and then you can stay for tea.'

'I haven't had my cuddle with Ben.' The big tabby was
stretched out on the futon, his paw raised towards Tally.

'Well, do that while I find my history exercise book. And
a pen.'

Tally lay with Ben. He purred. Watching John, Tally said,
'Can I see your questions?'

'Yes, but they are probably silly.'

'I'll hear them anyway when you read them out,' said Tally. 'Goodbye for the moment, Ben. See you soon.'

They walked up the street. 'I hope we don't see the man with the horrible face,' Tally said.

John knew about the man with the horrible face, but he did not quite believe in him. 'I bet we don't,' he said.

But Tally was not distracted, and added sombrely, 'In his horrible car.'

They rang the doorbell of Number One.

Beale, looking out of his window on the opposite side of the street, saw them and wondered what they were doing. He hoped they had not identified Mr Packington as a Criminal or a Victim. 'Harry,' said Beale, 'can you cast any light on why Tally and John are ringing Mr Packington's doorbell?'

Harry thought. 'What it might be,' he said, 'is to ask him about the Second World War. You do it in History in the first term at Jibbs. At least, we did. It was really difficult to find anyone to interview, though two people had great grand-fathers. I didn't have anyone. You were saying Mr Packington fought in it. So maybe.'

Beale was satisfied, but went on watching Number One until the door was opened. A woman opened the door. 'That's the daughter, I think,' said Beale. 'Good. I'm glad she's there.'

John explained his enterprise to Isabel Packington. He finished by saying, 'It's only five questions.'

'Come in,' said Isabel, thinking this encounter might amuse Dad, or pass the time for him, anyway. She vaguely thought of offering the children refreshment, but could not cope with what and how. She led them into the sitting-room. 'Dad,' she said, 'these two young people –' she ascertained their names – 'John and Tally, would like to ask you some questions about the war, for school. Is that all right?'

Max Packington, silent and polite, looked at John and Tally as they sat down. It was a very kind look, Tally thought, but John found it awe-inspiring. It was up to him to begin, and he glanced at Tally, and then said, 'Excuse me, Mr Packington, but how old were you when you went into the war?'

Isabel managed not to answer for her father, so a minute passed. John was afraid it was a rude question.

'Eighteen,' said Max Packington. 'I think that's right. Eighteen.'

John wrote. He now thought all five of the questions he had made up were silly, but he ploughed on, his face scarlet, writing the answers in the spaces he had provided under the questions. 'Did you kill anyone?'

There was another silence, and they all looked at Max. Not even Isabel knew the answer to this, though as a child she had wondered.

'Yes,' said Max.

'You don't look it, Mr Packington,' Tally said.

'Thank you, my dear,' said Max to Tally.

'Three. Did you ever nearly die?' asked John.

'It depends what you mean. There were a lot of bullets and grenades and shells. If they had hit me I would have died. But they didn't.'

'Did they hit other people?' asked Tally. John gave her a worried look because this was not one of the five questions.

'Yes,' said Max.

'Lots and lots?' This was Tally again.

'Yes.'

'What was the worst thing about the war?' cut in John, embarrassed, reading from his list.

Max thought, but could not answer. Then he said, 'Everything.'

'What was the best thing?' John had reached the fifth and last question.

Again Max thought. 'The best thing for me,' he said, 'was it decided me to become a doctor.'

John wrote, and closed his History exercise book. 'Thank you,' he said.

'I expected you to say the best bit was when you were decorated,' said Isabel, who had expected no such thing, but wanted to get this detail in for the children.

'Decorated?' said the children, who had not heard the word in this context.

'By the King. For courage. Would you like to see the medal?'

'No,' said Max firmly. 'No more about that. It was shameful.'

'Shameful?' exclaimed Isabel. Then, to the children, who were puzzled, 'It's a great honour.'

'Shameful,' reiterated Max. 'All the bravest men had been killed.'

A silence greeted this, as well it might. Tally stopped swinging her foot. John stared at the floor. Then he stood up, and said, 'Thank you very much. We'll go now, if that's all right.'

~

Isabel went to get a cup of tea. 'I hope you enjoyed that,' she said, putting the cup down beside Max.

'Enjoyed what?' asked Max.

'That visit. The children.'

But it had gone. Max had learned not to ask questions. He did not want it to be known that he was remembering less and less. But he could not help being curious. What visit? What children? It would have been nice to know.

Isabel's thoughts were turning more and more to a live-in carer. She wondered if Max might prefer a man to a woman.

146

She had always imagined a woman, but perhaps a man might be easier for him. In the end, some sort of full-time care would be essential. She knew Max did not remember the children's visit, and this frightened her. She knew it frightened him as well. Often she did not say things because she knew she would see him fail to understand, and then not want to ask. And then he would stare out of the window, sad-faced, secretly puzzling. Thus at the moment she did not say, 'Laurence is definitely coming over after Christmas,' in case she saw Max wondering silently who Laurence was. She dreaded that for herself and for Max.

'This can't go on for ever,' she thought. Always now, when she let herself in to the house with her key, and came quietly into the sitting-room, she had the fantasy that she might see Max dead in his chair. She liked the idea that there would be a photo album on his lap, and that it would be open at a picture of her mother. He would have died in peace. What a relief it would be. A relief for her and, certainly, a relief for him.

Perhaps the cleaner, Josie, who was single despite being known as Mrs Gray, might be persuaded to move in as a carer. She was not trained, but that perhaps did not matter. Max knew her, and he might not realise she was living in. He would simply suppose it was always Tuesday, which was the day she came in to clean. Isabel determined to canvass this with Josie Gray. Something must be done.

Isabel wondered and sometimes worried about Max's visits to the Viscount Palmerston at the other end of the street. She had heard about these outings from neighbours – Beale and Sally Pace, who lived at Number Eighteen, and were very nice and caring; and, further down the road on the opposite side to Max, Anne and Eric Darwin, who were also nice; Eric claimed to be an ex-patient of Max's. Max was lucky in his neighbours, thought Isabel. There always seemed to be somebody to notice if he looked lost in the street, and tactfully come to the rescue. It would be awful to deprive him of his freedom. It had not come to that yet. However, he was certainly deteriorating.

The worst thing that had happened so far was when, one day last week, Max had turned up in a taxi at his hospital, and tried to make his way to the heart department, telling everyone he met that he was late for his clinic. The hospital had been largely rebuilt, so he was completely lost. Someone took him to Cardiology, assuming he was a patient, and there it dawned on an elderly nurse and a doctor who had been his student who he was, and they told him his clinic had been cancelled for today. They sat him down and gave him tea, and, when he was calmer, deputed a nurse to take him home in a taxi. They had a bit of trouble discovering his address, but Isabel had entered 'daughter' after her name on his mobile phone, so they phoned her, and she had to leave work to be at Max's house to receive him. Max was silent and worried when he arrived, his scanty white hair on end, and Isabel suspected he had some memory of the episode, perhaps briefly, but there was no way of telling.

But, of course, Max *could* remember the past. He liked photo albums. After the hospital adventure, Isabel had withdrawn the DVDs of heart operations and substituted the family albums. Max had not shown signs of noticing or regretting the transition. But he never seemed to want to turn the album pages on his own. Isabel had to be there. Or perhaps, thought Isabel, Josie Gray.

~

John and Tally were eating tea.

'It's not fair on Harry,' said Tally. 'He just has tea at our house and we have this lovely, lovely tea.'

Anne was pleased. 'Well,' she said, 'I'm sure he knows he's always welcome.'

Eric came into the room. With a pantomime of greed and acquisitiveness he took one of the children's buttered buns. 'Nothing better than a buttered bun,' he said. '*Mieux que toute la haute cuisine du monde.*'

'*Oui,*' said John. He did not like talking French with Eric, but he knew Eric meant well.

Anne was speaking to Eric. 'You know the French students opposite,' she said. 'At last the parents have been over and collected poor Marie-Christine. She was on crutches walking out to the car. I think it's criminal that she's been left so long to the tender mercies of Jean-Luc and the other laddie.'

John and Tally exchanged glances. John mouthed the word 'criminal' to Tally.

'Was Marie-Christine a victim, in a way?' Tally asked Anne, looking at John.

'In a way she was, though I don't think any harm was intended.'

'What are you two giggling about?' asked Eric.

'Nothing,' they said. To change the subject John said, 'We went to see Mr Packington to ask him about the war.'

Anne and Eric were both interested. 'I wonder how old he is,' said Anne to Eric.

'Eighty-six,' said Tally, who had done the sum. 'He answered all John's questions. He was really nice.'

'He didn't care about his medal, and being decorated,' said John. 'He thought it was shameful, because all the bravest men had been killed.'

'Did you know he fixed my heart?' said Eric.

'The war made him become a doctor,' said Tally.

'I'll show you the scar, some time,' said Eric.

'Why isn't he Doctor Packington?' John asked.

149

'Because he's a surgeon. That makes you Mister,' said Eric. 'Is Georgia coming over tonight?' he asked Anne.

'Yes. She thinks she will finish the picture. Or nearly.'

'What picture?' asked Tally.

Anne regretted mentioning it. 'Oh . . .' she said.

'I'll show you,' said John. 'It's really brilliant.' He took Tally next door. Tally could be heard exclaiming, 'Wow', and, 'Brilliant', and, 'Is it really by Georgia?'

'Now it'll be all over the street,' said Eric to Anne. 'It's your fault, mentioning it in front of the children.'

'It doesn't matter,' said Anne serenely. 'Why shouldn't someone paint a portrait of someone?'

'Yes, but . . .' With the children out of the room, Eric pinched another bun. What he could not say was that in every contour and every brush stroke of Georgia's painting love could be perceived. Anne knew this was what he meant. She turned to the sink, for tears were in her eyes.

~

Hugh and Mel had just finished supper when they heard the doorbell. Mel went to answer it. On the doorstep stood Finola Hodgkins from Number Ten.

Mel had never taken to Finola Hodgkins, a small, sprightly woman slightly younger than herself who lived exactly opposite, but that might have been because Finola had a baby and Mel did not. Finola and Barry Hodgkins, being another young professional couple, would have seemed ideal people for Mel and Hugh to make friends with, yet this had never happened. But now, on the doorstep, here was Finola.

'No, I won't come in,' she said. 'I just wanted to say how pleased I am for you about the baby, that's wonderful. I've got a lot of baby clothes, Chloe's, so when you get nearer the time, we can go through them and see what you'd like.'

'But you'll want them,' said Mel. 'You will probably have another.'

'If that happens I can come back to you for anything that hasn't worn out,' laughed Finola. 'And it seems silly, living opposite, that we never see each other. Perhaps you could come in for a drink one evening, or come to supper.'

'Yes,' said Mel, and Finola departed.

Mel stormed into the kitchen. 'Hugh,' she said, 'how does Finola Hodgkins know about the baby? If she knows, everyone in the street must know. I never wanted . . . I never expected . . . I haven't even told Mum yet.'

'It must be me,' said Hugh. 'I intimated something to Beale Pace. Only intimated. Well, he sort of guessed. Oh dear.'

'What if I have a miscarriage?' said Mel. 'Nobody ever tells people till the third month.'

'The third month?' said Hugh, astonished.

'It's really annoying,' said Mel.

Hugh could see that it was, and did not know how to make it better. 'I'm terribly sorry,' he said.

'Here's Finola Hodgkins, who we hardly know, offering me Chloe's baby clothes.'

'Is that who it was at the door?'

'Yes.'

Mel came close to Hugh and grabbed both his ears. 'You fool!' she said, pulling them, but not hard. Hugh was penitent, but baffled as to how the news had got around.

～

Beale had mentioned it to Sally, more to boast about his own powers of intuition than because he thought it would be of any interest to her. Within the next few days there had been a Mothers' Meeting outside Anne's, and Sally had let it slip. Anne had nobly said nothing of it to anybody; but Maria Garcia, excited about her own new pregnancy, which, indeed, was how the topic had come up, had told Juan, and Juan, assuming it was common knowledge, had passed it on to Finola and Barry along with the news of his own baby.

'And now we've got to be friends with the Hodgkins!' wailed Mel. 'We've got to have drinks, dinner even, and with them just opposite, it's altogether too close! We'll have to move house!'

'They may be very nice,' Hugh ventured.

'You know they read the *Telegraph*.'

'Don't be so hidebound. We'll need baby-sitters. And anyway on closer acquaintance they may dislike us intensely.'

Mel went into the garden. She stood and regarded the peaceful autumn evening, but there was no peace in her heart. Before she was pregnant, among her daydreams had been one of buying baby clothes. It was not a daydream she approved of, because of a certain vulgarity she discerned in it or attributed to it, but there it had been. She had noticed baby-wear in shops, and desired beyond words to have the need to make purchases. There were displays she had turned away from in tears. And now she was to have Chloe's cast-offs instead. To make matters worse, Mel could not stamp and shout about it to Hugh, who probably thought Finola's offer generous and pleasingly community-minded. And, of course, that was the right response.

After a few minutes Hugh came out and put his arms round her. 'Don't let anything spoil anything,' he said. He rocked her. His cheek was touching hers. 'Be careful not to let anything spoil anything.'

She relaxed. 'It's hormones,' she said. 'Well, not entirely. The fact that you let the cat out of the bag isn't hormones.'

Hugh wanted to defend himself but resisted. 'I was careless,' he said. 'There's no excuse and I'm sorry.' They stood in the garden. He tightened his arms around her. Then he said, 'It's getting chilly. We'd better go in. It's good that the baby will be born in July. Nice and warm.'

Chapter 14

If Eric thought that Anne and Georgia's idea of going to church together on one or two Sunday mornings was exclusively to annoy him, he was mistaken. Anne's family of origin was religious, though only to a conventional degree; Georgia's was more agnostic, but she had been sent to a church school. Thus both women were familiar with the Church of England, albeit from decades ago, and neither disliked it. Resonances from readings still sometimes rang in their ears. In all the time each had lived in the street, neither had set foot in St Sebald's, close though it was, nor had it crossed their minds to do so; but once they did think of it, in conversation together, they felt attracted and curious. The important thing for them, of course, was that it was a shared interest and a joint activity. They had discovered at the time of Brenda's death that each other's company was fun, and funny, and joyful in a different way from anything else in their lives, whether they were looking for a crematorium or chasing a cat; and anything they did together ever since, including the portrait, had been delightful. So off they went one Sunday morning to a service, and stood shoulder to shoulder, remembering or not remembering the various prayers and hymns, attempting to sing or failing to do so, and looking forward to discussing the exploit on the short walk home, which they did, with their usual mixture of seriousness and companionable hilarity. They had no illusions that they would keep it up. It was a version of truancy for Anne, in whom the rituals of Sunday lunch were ingrained, and after a few weeks Eric breathed again.

Another reason, besides the pleasure of doing something together, that Anne and Georgia were drawn to attending church was that at this point both felt in need of strength. Their impending separation hung heavily on their spirits. They had not talked about its momentousness, and in consequence each suffered privately. They had not talked about it because such a conversation, if it happened, would touch inescapably on the fact that they loved each other, which had never quite been said. Both felt a little better for the church venture. The language of suffering and sacrifice, of loss, endurance and hope, gathered them into experience which is universal, and which richly acknowledges the pain of human life.

Now, the portrait was finished. The last fold of the patchwork on Anne's lap, and the last loose patch in the basket beside her were meticulously coloured and shaded. A picture which had been so loved in the making became something different, albeit still loved, when an artefact. Anne got over her shyness about showing it off, and all who came to the house provided their quota of disbelief and delight. Georgia became proud of it and took photographs. Eric considered its glazing. It was square, two feet by two feet, and many were the moments recently when Georgia had wished it bigger, although at the beginning, in its blankness, it had seemed enormous. Anne's expression was kind, humorous and engaged, and her grey hair dishevelled. She looked surprised to be taken so much notice of, as well she might; and there was some self-deprecation in her face. Her hands were wrinkled and work-hardened, women's hands, old hands, and the right one held the needle with great delicacy.

'It's for you, you have it,' said Georgia, wanting it herself. Anne demurred, much though she wanted it. They postponed deciding which house it would be in, and anyway, Georgia pointed out that they could easily transport it up and down the street if desired. Anne would have it on her wall for the moment, until Georgia came home from Sinai. To leave the matter like that pleased them both, making Georgia's safe return sooner and more ordinary.

'You should be a professional,' said Sally Pace. 'Honestly. You're wasted on the snails.'

'You should paint the Queen,' said Maria Garcia.

Hugh said, 'When you're back from your travels, will you paint Mel? For a fee, of course.'

But Georgia felt like a knight who has laid his sword at the feet of his lady and cannot use it otherwise. So she laughed and pretended not to take the compliments seriously.

The process that began, shaped and completed the portrait had covertly expressed Anne and Georgia's feelings for each other. Now that the process was over, there was a question, unspoken, in Anne's case unformulated, as to whether they would find a different language, or whether their love would be struck dumb. Georgia felt the time had come for a declaration, and as the one with more experience of charting the life of the heart, she thought the initiative lay with her.

Anne was to come to Georgia's to be taught how to look after the vivarium. November had arrived, the month of Georgia's departure. It was a grey and drizzly morning. Georgia looked out of her window, waiting for Anne. Roland and Beatrice kept their big front window closed now. Georgia did not know how Beatrice managed her smoking. Perhaps she had given up. They were shadowier figures for Georgia with the window shut. Beatrice had had her hair cut, and had accordingly lost glamour for Georgia. The wave between

Georgia and Beatrice had not been repeated. It would not be now. Essentially Roland and Beatrice belonged to the epoch before Georgia had fallen in love with Anne. They would be gone before Georgia returned.

Now Georgia saw the door of Max Packington's house open. She expected to see Max or the daughter, whose name she did not know. Instead she saw a small, aproned figure, shaking out a mat. She watched. Did Max have dementia? Street encounters with him had led both Georgia and Anne to wonder. Georgia hoped he was not suffering, though it seemed likely that he was. Who would not be, in that plight? Then Georgia spotted Anne, in an unattractive, see-through mac, hurrying up the street, and, watching her, a smile appeared and broadened on Georgia's face.

They went straight into the garden.

'I'm not going to take notes this time,' said Anne. 'This is just preliminary. You'll have to show me a lot of times to make sure I get it right.'

'It's not hard,' said Georgia. They stood in front of the large plastic structure. 'Can you see any snails?'

Anne looked. 'No.'

'That's because it's cold. If it warms up after this drizzle, they'll come out. Now, this is where you spray the water. You don't want too much. Some rain gets in through these holes here, anyway. If it's pelting, I actually cover the vivarium – with that plastic sheet. They like it damp, not sodden. Try squirting this yourself.'

Anne tried and succeeded. 'How many squirts?'

'Up to ten can't hurt. You fill the chamber of the spray gun at that tap. This is the little lid.' Anne craned to see the little lid, and Georgia went on, 'More water in the summer, but it won't be summer.'

'What about food?'

'This is their food, and there's a tub in the shed. You can scatter that. Just a small trowelful'.

'Where's the trowel?'

'In the tub. But what they really like are leaves. I get Cos lettuce or Little Gem. It's better for them if they have the sort of leaves that stay crisp for a while.'

'How much a day?'

'Say eight leaves. Less if they are big. But you won't need to do them every day.'

'No, but I will. Now I can see two snails,' said Anne. 'Different colours.'

'There are two different species in here,' said Georgia. 'Aspersa, those are the tabbies, and you see more of them in London gardens than any other species. And Hortensis, with those pretty, yellowish stripey shells. They're both common English varieties. I'm following up in the vivarium whether they seem to see any difference, themselves, between their two sub-species.'

'How can you tell?'

'Lots of ways, but choice of sexual partners is one way. But we have to wait for the mating season for that.'

'Imagine if Eric could see me,' said Anne. 'Taking snails seriously, instead of stamping them out.'

'Does it make you feel disloyal?'

'Not a bit. I haven't killed a snail since you told me what your work is.'

'Does he know you're looking after the vivarium for me?'

'Yes. He'll probably come along and have a look,' said Anne, who did not want him to.

They stood up from their stooped positions in the cold and the drizzle, Georgia coatless, Anne in her transparent mac, their hair shining with tiny raindrops, and looked at each other.

'I love you,' said Georgia, 'as I am sure you know.'

'Yes,' said Anne. 'And I love you. I have never known anyone like you. In nearly seventy years.'

They did not say any more than that, nor did they feel the need to. They went into the house, and over coffee smiled a lot and were happy, but talked of other matters – the vivarium; the Christmas holiday plans for John; Georgia's travels.

~

Eric went to the window to see if the vehicle he had just heard could have anything to do with a delivery he was expecting from the wine shop. A car was hurrying away up the street, and, as it was irrelevant to what Eric had hoped, he began to turn away from the window. Then he turned back. He went right up to the window and peered out, gripped by dread. 'Anne,' he said, without moving.

'What's the matter?' said Anne. She joined him at the window. Together they stared down at a point in the gutter on their side of the pavement. As one, they moved out of the sitting-room to the front door and into the street. 'Oh no,' said Anne. It was as they feared. Benn lay in the gutter. 'Is he dead?' she whispered.

Eric stooped and investigated. 'Yes, I think so,' he said. 'Yes, he is.' Eric was moved, and did not want to show it. 'Get something to wrap him in,' he said crisply. While Anne was gone Eric knelt down. He touched the warm tabby fur and choked.

Anne came back with a white, fleecy bath towel. She folded it and laid it on the pavement. Eric got his hands under Benn's floppy body and lifted him carefully on to the towel, hoping bits would not come apart. They did not, for externally Benn's body was uninjured by the impact. Eric wrapped him in the towel, then carried him into the house. Anne was at his heels, shocked and openly crying.

It was easier indoors, where they had no fear of interruption. Eric laid Benn down on a low table in the sitting-room. Anne sat beside him. Eric stood. After a minute, Eric went to fetch a damp cloth. 'That's blood round his mouth,' he said. 'We must wipe it away before the children see him.' He wiped, as gently as if Benn were alive. The thought of the children made Anne cry afresh. When Eric had wiped away the blood, he tried to dry the fur he had wetted. 'Some bloody road hog,' he said. 'Must have been going too fast.'

Benn's eyelids were half-closed, and there was some dust stuck to what could be seen of his eyes. His mouth was a little open, showing his teeth. His front paws were tucked up tidily together.

'How old would he be?' Eric asked.

'Georgia would know how long Brenda had him. Quite a long time I think. I think he's had a good innings, and a happy life.'

'And he can't have felt a thing.'

Anne wanted to ring Georgia, but did not like to risk Eric feeling sidelined, when he was so involved, an involvement which did not surprise Anne, but which pleased her, and made her love him. However, Georgia rang, and it fell to Eric to tell her the bad news. 'Georgia's coming over,' Eric said to Anne as he put down the phone. Anne sat by Benn, but she did not like to touch him. Georgia had no such difficulty, and stroked him goodbye in a friendly, matter-of-fact way. She lifted his chilling body to arrange the towel more closely and symmetrically around him, so that he looked cosy and nested, which might make it less awful for John. She did not cry, in case her tears led Anne to think that she harboured unshareable feelings about Brenda, which she did not.

Eric came back into the room and greeted Georgia. He asked her how long Brenda had had Benn, and that gave them something to try to work out. The conclusion was that Benn was probably about nine, which was not too bad; but in another way it was, for until today he was a cat in his prime. They sighed, and looked at him, and said the same things again, that nine was not a bad life-span for a cat; that his life had been happy; that he had not suffered in death, though each found that hard to believe, for there would have been a moment, surely, of horror and incredulity. Then Anne introduced the idea that he was spared old age and decrepitude, which might have stemmed partly from the private thought that she was spared his old age and decrepitude. This contribution was welcome, too. Eric explained that, from the appearance of the corpse, the car must have struck him, rather than run him over, and it was the impact that killed him, and this was why he would not have felt a thing.

'But there was blood coming out of his mouth,' said Anne.

'Internal injuries,' said Eric. 'From the impact. Some road hog driving too fast.'

They were all trying to make it as good as possible. All three contemplated the suddenness of the death; that this morning Benn was exactly as always, and now would never stir again; but they did not express these thoughts, as being too banal.

~

At ten past four the inevitable happened, and John's key was heard in the door. Georgia had tactfully gone home, so that Anne and Eric could cope with this together. Anne hurried to the door and met him.

'What's the matter?' asked John.

'It's Benn,' said Anne, Eric appearing behind her.

'What? Not dead?'

Both grandparents nodded, and tears began to slide down

John's face. They were the first tears he had shed in this house that were not tears of homesickness. 'Is he . . .?'

'Yes.' They led him into the sitting-room. To while away the time since Georgia had left, Anne had placed a few small late-flowering blooms from the garden by Benn's head.

There was a sharp intake of breath from John. 'Oh Ben,' he whispered.

'We're so sorry,' said Anne. 'We know he was a special friend of yours.'

'He came to us about the same time as you did,' said Eric. He blew his nose. 'It was a car.'

John had his telephone out. He was dialling. 'Tally,' he said huskily, 'Ben's dead.'

Tally was at the house before it seemed possible, with no shoes on. John was waiting for her at the front door. He led her into the sitting-room, which in the course of the day had taken on the hushed quality of a shrine. Tally leaned over Benn and kissed him between the ears. Her tears were pouring on to his fur and she was sobbing. She picked him up and held him. 'He's hard,' she said, 'he's cold. Oh, poor poor Ben.' She pressed her face against him and kissed his eyes, his nose, his mouth. She put him in his towelling nest again, and laid her cheek against him. He was wet with her tears. John, standing beside her, was crying, partly for Benn, partly for Tally. Eric's nose trumpeted again. Anne was wiping her eyes, but had emotional space to be a little worried about hygiene.

'What happened?' John asked, and the story was told afresh.

'He wouldn't have felt a thing,' said Eric.

'He would,' said Tally. 'He would have felt death.'

'He wouldn't have had time to,' said Eric.

But the thought that he would have felt death led Tally to pick him up again and kiss his face, his ears and his paws. 'His nose is dry,' she said. 'Poor, poor little Ben.'

'He had a good life,' said Eric.

'We'll have to bury him, Tally,' said John.

'Yes,' said Tally, and laid him down again in his nest. 'Just this morning,' she said, and from her the thought was far from banal, 'he must have thought it was a perfectly normal day.'

'He was in the front to say goodbye to me when I started for school this morning,' said John. 'Little did I know . . .' Unlike Tally's, his grief was not too raw for sentimentality to have a part in it. 'Little did I know it was the last time. Little did he know.'

There was a silence, while both children stroked Benn, Tally his head and ears, John his hindquarters. Eric cleared his throat. 'I've dug a grave for him,' he said, 'in a nice bit of the garden.'

'He must have a good funeral,' said Tally. 'He was such a good cat.'

'Shall we do that now?' suggested Anne, who was not sure that she wanted a dead cat in the middle of the sitting-room all night. And into tomorrow, which was also a school day. So twenty-four hours more, at least.

'We have to get Harry,' said Tally. 'He knew Ben.'

'And Georgia,' said Anne.

Georgia arrived on the doorstep at the same time as Harry and Beale. 'Poor old Ben,' said Harry. He had a lump in his throat, but no intention of crying. 'There he is.'

'A car, I suppose?' said Beale. 'What a shame.'

'They should put speed humps in the street,' said Eric. 'He must have been going too fast. They do, often. They should put speed humps in the street.'

'If everyone's here,' said Anne, 'perhaps we could go out into the garden.'

'Wait a minute,' said Tally. 'Come with me, John.' John did not know where they were going, but ran up the road behind

Tally, Harry following, mildly curious. They got to the front door of Number One, and Tally rang the bell. Max Packington appeared.

'Mr Packington,' said Tally. 'Our cat's been run over. Will you come to his funeral?'

Max checked his jacket pocket for keys and reached for his stick. He was ready. The procession made its way slowly down the street, Tally beside Max, John and Harry behind. When it arrived at Eric and Anne's, it found the party standing uncertainly in the sitting-room. No one knew what the children had run off for, and some were concerned that Tally had no shoes on. Max was welcomed by the grown-ups, and the group of eight began to move into the garden. Tally went first, carrying Benn, handsomely shrouded in fluffy white. This was the moment at which Anne knew for sure that she must say farewell to one of her good towels, and she was glad no one knew she had even had such a thought. When they arrived at the deep, square hole Eric had dug, they arranged themselves around it.

Eric took Benn from Tally's arms. 'It's all right, Tally,' he said, and she had to relinquish him. Eric was not quite sure how to manage the interment, while preserving the dignity of the occasion. He put Benn at the side of the grave. The breeze ruffled his fur. Then Eric lay down, and from that level could place Benn decorously at the bottom of the grave. Then he stood up, brushing down his clothes.

There was a pile of earth and a spade nearby. Eric picked up the spade. 'Ready?' he asked. They all watched and all heard the cold clods fall on to Benn, more and more, until he was invisible. Tally cried uncontrollably, and went to Beale, who put his arm round her. John was crying, but went to no one, and Anne it was who came behind him and tried to give him a hug.

They turned to go indoors. 'We'll make him a gravestone,' John said to Tally.

Her face brightened. 'Tomorrow,' she said. 'After school.' Then, 'Are you glad I invited you, Mr Packington?'

'Yes,' said Max. 'Thank you. I think it was because of death.'

'It was,' said Tally.

Chapter 15

'So will you be arriving on the third?' Isabel asked Laurence.

'Yes, all being well.'

'What do you mean, all being well? Haven't you got your ticket yet?'

'Yes, I've got that.'

'So you will be. And staying for three weeks.'

'Yes, or possibly a bit less.'

'You can stay with me, you know. Remember we've got Josie Gray living in with Dad now.'

'How is she getting on?'

'Well. It's certainly light-touch regulation from her. But perhaps that's the best. She doesn't keep a tight rein on his comings and goings. She wouldn't know how to. But she's there. If he's forgotten his keys she'll open the door. He wanders about, rather. But he always seems to get home, or someone brings him home. He's got good neighbours. Meanwhile Mrs Gray does his meals and keeps things going in the house. She's a good cook, so he is eating, and that's important.'

'How are his spirits?'

'He talks about death. He says he has outlived his generation. And it's true. He doesn't have any friends his age. You'd think he might. Eighty-six isn't very old these days. But he's unlucky there. If you think of Mum and Dad's friends, they're all dead. Or one or two, disabled, in distant old folks' homes, and probably battier than Dad.'

'Does he want to die?'

'Yes, I think he does. I caught him stethoscoping himself the other day. When he saw me come in, he looked embarrassed, then he said, "So terribly old, but not enough wrong with me yet to die." I asked him if he wanted to die. He said, "I don't want to be depressing, darling, but of course I do. I'm losing my mind, and it's getting worse." So he does know. He does suffer. I said, "You aren't losing your mind, you are losing your short-term memory." He looked at me and smiled and shook his head sadly, as if we could both see through that euphemism. I was choked. I often am.'

'When you think,' said Laurence. 'When you think what he was like.'

'Well, it's no good saying that. And he's still got his courage. Think what it must be like, to know you are losing your mind. He's very brave, and never complains.'

'Does he see that Dr March?'

'He's got pills from Dr March. As far as I know he takes them, but he doesn't want to see him. I can't make him.' Now Isabel got annoyed, as so often in conversations with her brother. 'Perhaps you will be able to make him, when you are here.'

'He probably won't even know me,' said Laurence, to mollify, but also because it was probably true.

~

'We should do something about Josie Gray,' said Anne to Eric.

'Who on earth is Josie Gray?' Eric looked up from sand-papering a square piece of board. He had spread newspaper to catch the sawdust.

'Josie Gray at Number One. She looks after Max Packington.

I think she's lonely and anxious and rather out of her depth. She's never been a carer. She's not trained.'

'What should we do?'

'We can have them to supper, Max and Josie Gray. And Georgia can come too.'

'Well, I've no objection.' Eric held up his piece of board to see if there were rough patches. 'Good enough?' he asked Anne.

She crossed the room to inspect. 'Good enough,' she said. They both contemplated it for a moment. It was the wood for Benn's gravestone. The children had decided on the inscription, but Eric was to transfer the words on to a piece of wood, and devise a way of making the gravestone stand firmly on the grave.

'What are the words?' Anne asked.

Eric took a piece of paper out of his pocket and showed it to Anne.

HERE LIES
BEN DARWIN
A GOOD CAT
TERRIBLY MISSED

'Should you change the spelling of Ben?' Anne wondered.

'I should. I've told the children. They didn't mind at all. John googled Tony Benn and they read about him and they were rather pleased, I think. Now I'll go out to the shed where I've got some white paint.' He looked at his newspaper and sawdust.

'Don't worry, I'll pick all that up. You're a good man, Eric, and a good grandfather.'

~

169

Beale was clearing and sweeping as usual after his family's breakfast when he heard the doorbell. He pulled on some underpants and went to the door. When he saw the figure on the doorstep he wished he had pulled on a bit more, for, in spite of basic standards of decency being met, he realised she was taken aback by such an abundance of male flesh suddenly so close to her. However, she pulled herself together, and said, 'I'm knocking on all the doors. It's the doctor. I don't know where he's got to.'

'The doctor? Come in.'

'No, I'm going on. I just wonder if anyone's seen him this morning.' She was looking up and down the street as she spoke. She was small and rather fragile-looking, at least seventy, thought Beale.

'And you are?' he asked.

'Mrs Gray, the housekeeper. I'll have to ring Isabel if he doesn't turn up soon.'

Beale put two and two together. 'You mean Mr Packington. If Mr Packington doesn't turn up soon.'

'Yes, the doctor.'

'You go on looking, Mrs Gray,' said Beale. 'I'll put on some clothes and join you in the search.'

Beale was enlivened to have an unexpected project, but, disappointingly, by the time he was dressed and on his doorstep, he saw Max Packington and Mrs Gray walking together towards Max's house. He thought for a minute of accosting them, but decided against. Where Max had been, or why, no one would ever know, least of all himself.

~

That evening, when Beale came in from Pam's, Sally was sitting in front of the TV, her shoes off, her legs curled up under her. She had not bothered to change out of her smart suit.

Normally she would have worried about the smart suit taking on unwelcome contours from this posture. She was dozing over a programme in which penises underwent disastrous consequences from plastic surgery, and in front of her was the easy crossword with a few words put in. When she looked round at Beale, the word 'unkempt' came into his mind. The sight of her like this made something hurt inside Beale.

'Just going for our whiskies,' he said. He was taking a decision. He came back and sat down beside her. He turned off the penises.

'Darling,' he said. 'I want to ask you a very important question. Would you rather I gave up Pam's?'

'Why do you ask that?'

'Because you look a bit like a human derelict. I mean compared with your usual appearance.'

'Well, I've been at home since eight, you went straight out, it's now a quarter to twelve, my spirits have been low for hours.' Sally had been looking forward to her whisky, and took a big swallow. 'And it's the third evening this week. How come you are always needed?'

Beale did not want to tell Sally the truth, which was that his presence as a barman enhanced the atmosphere and increased the attendance at Pam's. So he did not answer that question, but said, 'If I stop working at Pam's, we will be five hundred pounds odd down every week. How worth having is that, compared to other factors?'

Sally was silent. She was not used to thinking of money matters as secondary. 'It's been a help,' she said. 'Hasn't it?'

'Yes,' said Beale.

'Also,' said Sally reluctantly, 'you like it. You love it. We can't get over that. Why the company of that bloody Cath . . .'

'It's not her. It's the people. It's the old boys, at their tables alone. Mr Packington occasionally, others more often. Young couples. The middle-aged. The banter. The group round the bar. The big football screen, sometimes.'

'It's being liked, I know you.'

'It is indeed, you do.'

'Including liked by Cath.'

'Yes. Everyone likes me. Even Mel Davis is friendly now; she and Hugh sometimes come in. Listen, darling, there is no hanky-panky with Cath. Even if I fancied her, which I don't, I would have to be mad. The whole street would know. We would have to move house.'

Sally was comforted by the clear-sightedness of this. 'I know,' she said.

'The point is neither you nor I like being alone in the evening,' went on Beale. 'I used to be alone, when you came home late and then worked. Now it's your turn. The trouble with both of us is we don't have hobbies or interests, really. We rely on company.'

'At least I was in the house,' said Sally, 'even if I was working.'

'It doesn't make that much difference. I had to fall back on TV breasts and penises just as you have.'

There was a silence, then Sally said, 'It's nice of you to ask me if I'd rather you didn't do Pam's, because it consigns you afresh to being the lonely one. I could try to bring less work home. But would we go back to boozing and quarrelling?'

'I'm not sure, we'd have to see.'

'Suppose,' said Sally, 'suppose you just did Saturday night? Then I could brace myself and be ready and it would only be one night a week. And I would know in advance which one. At the moment your nights out get jumped on me, often when I haven't brought work home.'

'Yes, I know.'

Beale was being genuinely self-sacrificing, and Sally knew it. 'we say Friday and Saturday,' she said, 'and see how we go?'

'That will only be a couple of hundred pounds, and won't make much difference, money-wise,' said Beale. 'But that's not really the point, is it?'

'Not really. And I'll bring less work home.'

Sally did not say that much of the work that intruded into her leisure time was work directly for Ron that she should not really be doing. Thank goodness Ron had had his £5000 back, she thought, if she was going to cut down on this.

'Is that a decision?' asked Beale. 'You bring less work home, or do it on Friday and Saturday nights, and I cut down my pub work to those two nights?'

'You are being terribly nice,' said Sally.

'Ah, but I am terribly nice, remember,' said Beale.

'How will we manage not to quarrel, if we see so much more of each other?'

'We don't know if we will manage. Time will tell. Now let's have a few crossword clues, to settle our spirits before we go to bed.'

~

Mel had expected to be happy but she was miserable. For one thing she felt sick. She was a person who was not used to ill health of any sort, and had forgotten to take for granted that the first months of pregnancy, three at least, might create physical distress. She felt outraged. Her wonderful body was doing exactly what it was built for, but was further from wonderful than it had ever been in her life. She knew from her pregnancy books and from friends that all was exactly as it should be. That did not allay the outrage. The GP completely failed to cheer her up, although it was not Dr Meesdon. She cried. Hugh found her in tears, and was dismayed and at a loss.

'Haven't you been to work?' he asked, noting her jeans and general disarray.

'No. I didn't feel well enough.'

'Cup of tea?'

'Tea? Don't even mention the word.'

'Anything? A cheese biscuit?' These had gone down well recently, and he had bought a fresh supply.

'I never want to see a cheese biscuit let alone smell one ever again in my life.' Mel had to laugh at the vehemence of her reactions, and Hugh joined in the laugh. But Mel did not like that. 'It's no laughing matter,' she said. 'Imagine if you felt like this.'

'You have to eat, you know,' he said, hungry himself, and wanting to begin to cook a meal. 'Is there anything you could fancy?'

She thought long and deeply. 'A terribly small amount of mushrooms, sliced, not quartered, in white sauce, white sauce with a bit of parsley in it, the parsley finely chopped.'

'I think that can be managed,' said Hugh. 'I'll go to Sainsbury's for the parsley. We've got mushrooms.'

'No, don't you go. You cook. I'll go.' She returned with a bunch of parsley. 'It smells so wonderful,' she said.

'Good. I wonder if you could manage a little rice with your mushrooms.'

'I'll see.'

'I was thinking of a lamb chop. Could you face that?'

'No. And what's worse, I would have to go and sit in the garden if you are going to cook and eat a chop. Probably all night.'

'What about a bit of hard-boiled egg with rice and the mushrooms?' asked Hugh, after some thought.

'Could you bear hard-boiled egg instead of chop?'

'Yes, of course.'

'Well, I'll try.'

'Don't be too upset, sweetheart. At the end of all this is a baby. Remember that. A real live baby.'

Mel could not tell Hugh, but she was not sure she wanted

a real live baby. She had wanted to be pregnant. If she thought of childbirth, and a squalling baby such as her friends had, she felt trapped. She would be on maternity leave, and would be alone all day with a baby, Hugh at work. Suppose she did not like her new life? And how could she like it?

Far from wanting her pregnancy to be a secret, she now talked about it to anyone. Was there a part of her that wanted magically thus to bring on a miscarriage, talking about it in the first three months? At a Mothers' Meeting outside Anne's, her topic held the floor.

'Does everyone long to be pregnant then have cold feet?' she asked. 'That's what's happening to me. And I don't like to tell Hugh, after all the fuss I've made about wanting to get pregnant. And him so pleased for me.'

'I had all that,' said Sally. 'I was in my mid-thirties, and I thought it was my last chance. Then when I did get pregnant, I thought wow, what have I let myself in for? And I was right,' she added laughing, 'because it was Harry.'

'But Harry's wonderful,' said Mel.

'I know,' said Sally, who had been joking, or, probably, fishing for a compliment.

'I got pregnant before we meant to,' said Finola Hodgkins, 'and I thought the whole thing was scary and awful. But then I saw Chloe and everything came right. You'll see,' she added to Mel.

'I never wanted a baby specially,' said Anne. 'So I didn't really have any of this. I just found I was pregnant and got on with it. No agonies and ecstasies either way. Is that unusual?' No one knew, so Anne went on, to Sally, 'I've always wondered why you chose the name Heironimo.'

'It was a play Beale was in at the time. *Spanish Tragedy*? Something like that. Those were the glory days for Beale. Ah well.'

'I think I saw that,' murmured Georgia.

Talking with the women helped Mel, not so much to feel understood, which she was not sure she did, but to get rid of the sense that it was wrong to be ambivalent. She realised that the mention of Harry had helped, as well. In as little as twelve years, the pregnancy that was at present the size of a snail would be a tough and charming young person nearly as tall as herself in scruffy school uniform and with a head full of private dreams. The mention of Chloe also had its place. In less than three years the pregnancy would be chatty, ambitious and opinionated, intolerant of strangers and unfazed by such things as being knocked over by the family dog. Both these versions would have a look of Hugh, and that would be very interesting. Things did not have to be wondrous, thought Mel, to be worthwhile.

'You're looking unusually cheerful today,' said Hugh.

Chapter 16

Georgia's proposed trip was now generating a lot of emails. When the trip was planned and organised, Sinai had been perfectly safe. Now there were upheavals. Was the small international party of zoologists likely to be safe? Was it sensible to go? Should the expedition perhaps be postponed? Cancelled? The American professor who was the leader of the expedition remained confident. Was he in fact, too gung-ho? There were eleven participants altogether. They were now representing different shades of response. Emails from all of them came in, and emails from Georgia mingled with them.

Georgia wanted to go ahead, and gave her voice to that persuasion. The professor had been in touch with spokesmen from the Egyptian government and had been given the go-ahead. Two security guards were to be provided. Georgia was committed to the project, though she did see that she would not be able to be alone in a tent for a night listening for snails. That dream must go. Keeping together, under the care of the guards, surely the party would be all right. Meanwhile Georgia was aware of a bit of herself that would be relieved not to go because of Anne. Anne had admitted to hoping the trip would be cancelled, not selfishly, though the selfish motive was there and not denied, but because she was jumpy about Georgia's safety.

'There must be some danger,' said an email from a participant, 'or why would the government be providing us with guards? Who is paying for the guards, by the way?' Another said, 'I can assure everyone that there are no "hot spots" within hundreds of miles of where we are going. We are not going near any borders. People are worrying unnecessarily.' Another said, 'I agree Dr Fox. If we cancel and then everything remain peaceful, we regret.'

Georgia looked up from her computer and out of the window. She had not seen Roland or Beatrice recently. Now she spotted one of Brenda's nieces, the grey one, not the dyed one, coming out of Brenda's house. She could not resist running across the street to meet her. 'I haven't seen you or your sister for a long time,' she said.

'We had a young couple in there,' said the niece, 'just temporarily.' She was too annoyed to be sociable towards Georgia. 'They've gone. Just gone. Flitted.'

'What happened?'

'They paid for September, though it was blood out of a stone. They didn't pay for October, in spite of reminders. We were charging peanuts. We're more than halfway through November now. No, they've flitted. All their things are gone. Did you see anything?'

'I've seen them, of course. I mean I know who you mean. I didn't see them leave.'

'Well, that's it, I suppose. I must ring my sister. We'll probably start on the house now instead of after Christmas. It's all such a bother.'

Money for you, though, Brenda's money, thought Georgia as she went indoors. They must have been planning to flit. Or perhaps the urge to do so came on suddenly. Or indeed the financial need to do so. Where had they gone? Georgia recalled the hair, the cigarettes, the graceful poses half in and half out of the window. Beatrice appeared different now, calculating, no longer innocent. Roland, with his brisk, decisive movements and tight tee-shirts seemed even rascally. Georgia sighed and turned back to her emails.

'I suggest we all take out abduction insurance,' said a participant. 'It's a bit expensive, but you can shop around, and it makes a big difference if anything happens. It will give me peace of mind.' 'Thanks, I agree,' wrote Georgia. 'Good idea about abduction insurance. I didn't even know there was such a thing.' 'No harm of course,' chipped in someone else, 'but a complete waste of money. We are well out of any possible harm's way. You only have to look at the map.'

Georgia could not resist telephoning Anne, although they were meeting in the evening anyway. 'Roland and Beatrice have gone,' she said. 'Gone, owing rent.'

'I know, I just met Anthea Byfleet in a great state. She told me they left owing money. I nearly called them Roland and Beatrice! I just managed to stop myself.'

Georgia smiled. She liked the way Anne had taken up Roland and Beatrice, and it was amusing that you could never tell Anne anything about the street that she did not already know. 'Did she say their real names?'

'Yes, Kirk and Ita. I prefer Roland and Beatrice.'

'Kirk and Ita!'

'Let's stick to Roland and Beatrice.'

~

Tea-time at Anne and Eric's. Chicken, baked potatoes, green beans; chocolate brownies still warm.

'John, I got your tickets for Canada today,' said Anne.

'Canada?' cried Tally.

'Yes, for Christmas,' said John awkwardly. 'For the Christmas holidays.'

'Three weeks,' said Anne. 'Toronto airport.'

'You know, that's where my family are,' John reminded Tally.

'Yes, but I didn't know . . . Canada. Lucky!'

John was not sure. Lucky? He could imagine being homesick in Canada, homesick for the street.

Tally noticed the expression on his face, and said, 'Three weeks. That's not very long. It's a week today since Benn died, and it doesn't feel like any time at all. So only three of those.'

'It's okay,' said John. Somehow it wasn't.

'John,' whispered Tally.

'Yes?'

'Do you think it was the man with the horrible face that killed Benn?'

John pondered. 'But you say the man with the horrible face always drives slowly. The man who killed Benn was driving too fast.'

'Yes. My form at school are writing letters to the Council to ask for road humps in the street.'

'Are they?' John was always impressed by Tally's power, which had obviously in this instance been exercised over a teacher, as well as pupils. 'But no one in your form except you lives in the street.'

'That doesn't make any difference. They all know that it is where a cat died.'

~

Supper-time. Same menu, minus brownies which had been finished at tea. Georgia present.

'We must get around to asking Max Packington and Mrs Gray to supper,' said Anne. 'We've got to do that before you go.'

'Yes,' said Georgia. 'We'll fix a day.'

Anne turned to Eric. 'The young people at Number Twenty-three, Brenda's old house, have flitted.'

'I didn't know they were there,' said Eric. 'Is it flitted, or flat? It's sit and sat.'

'No one would understand what you meant if you said the young people have flat,' said Georgia, 'whichever it is, grammatically.'

'Any news about the expedition?' Anne asked Georgia.

'No new news. If anything seems dangerous, or if there are bad reports when we arrive, we can always abort the enterprise. We've said that. Or only the stoutest of heart will go on.'

'Which won't be you, I hope,' said Anne.

'Which won't be me.' They exchanged a smile.

'Snail academics abducted in Sinai,' said Eric. 'No news of where they are being held.'

Georgia smiled politely but Anne winced. 'I got John's tickets for Toronto today,' she said.

'We'll miss him,' said Eric.

'Anne, I've been thinking,' said Georgia. 'Do you mind if I cut your hair?'

Anne had a grey bun pulled back from her face, straggly at the front and sides. 'I'm not sure if I want short hair,' she said. 'If I had hair like yours I would.'

'I didn't mean that,' Georgia said. 'I think you'd look lovely with a fringe.'

'Okay,' said Anne.

After supper Anne fetched a towel, scissors, a brush and a comb and took her place on the chair so familiar from patchwork and from the portrait. She was smiling and slightly flushed. 'It reminds me of the portrait,' she said, taking off her glasses.

Georgia stood behind her and tenderly removed the battered clip and the combs from her hair. Then she pulled a chair into place and sat down squarely in front of Anne, her legs apart and her utensils in the lap of her skirt.

'What's happening?' asked Eric, from an armchair in a distant part of the room. 'It can't be another portrait.'

'Hair cutting. Hair styling,' said Georgia. She had been annoyed with Eric all evening. But then perhaps he was annoyed with her, she thought, and perhaps he had cause to be.

Georgia parted Anne's hair in the middle, and combed some locks forward. They descended over Anne's face. Georgia spent a bit of time seeking perfect symmetry, then began to cut. Anne heard the shearing noise with interest and affection. Georgia finished cutting, then combed the fringe and checked it again. She left it quite long; it was its nature to go in various directions. She did a little careful trimming. Finally she went behind Anne and brushed her hair and reclipped it. Then she sat on her chair again to stare at Anne.

The fringe modified the severity of Anne's face. It also hid forehead wrinkles. The same aspect of Anne as had been brought out in the portrait was discovered, emphasised and cherished. She could have been ten years younger, as she smiled at Georgia with a question in her eyes as to how she looked. The element of tiredness and doggedness that was often in her expression, a hint of gritted teeth and soldiering on, was nowhere to be seen.

'Mirror, Eric?' said Georgia.

'I don't know where there is one. Not one the right size.'

'There's one in the bathroom cupboard,' said Anne. 'Ordinary on one side, magnifying on the other.'

Georgia went for it. She gave it to Anne, who looked at herself with surprise and then delight. She touched her fringe gingerly, as if it might disappear, or might not be hers. Then she looked at Georgia. 'A new me,' she said.

Eric came across the room and peered at her. 'I'll have to watch out,' he said. 'You'll be going off with someone.' His sentiment, albeit facetious, caught something real about the change in Anne's appearance.

~

Almost before the street had got used to Anne's fringe, the day of departure came for Georgia. At half past seven in the morning Anne was at Georgia's door. The taxi for Heathrow was due at half past eight.

'What about John's breakfast?' Eric had said.

'You'll have to get it for him,' said Anne.

'But I'm not usually up at his breakfast time. I have to have some compensations for being retired.'

'I'm sure you'll get it for him. I'll put the basics out. He can get it for himself.'

'We never had Packington and Mrs Somebody to supper.'

'No. We didn't get round to that. We'll have to do it without Georgia.'

'One thing you don't have to worry about,' said Anne to Georgia, 'is the vivarium. I've got it absolutely taped, I've got notes, I've been through them, there's nothing I don't understand.'

'You're wonderful. You've got the key of the house?'

'Yes.'

'Wonderful. Now, if I make coffee, could you make things fit better in my case? The zip's almost impossible to close. In fact, it *is* impossible to close.'

Anne went into Georgia's bedroom and busied herself. 'It's all this camera stuff,' she called to Georgia after a few minutes.

'Yes, but I need all that. And the sound recording gear.'

'You're going to need a second case.'

'Am I? I feared as much.'

'You can have a mostly clothes case and a mostly gear case.'

Georgia came into the bedroom. 'This case,' she said, lifting a dusty one down from the top of the wardrobe. 'This'll do for the clothes.' Then she watched Anne, who was handling the incomprehensible electronics so respectfully and turning them this way and that for the best fit, and said, 'I love you very much.'

Anne looked up. 'And I love you.'

'You will be all right without me?'

'All right? Not really. But I'll survive. I'll be here when you get back.'

When Georgia came in with the coffee, she said, 'You won't worry about me, will you?'

'I'll try not to. I hope you'll be able to text, or email.' They had talked about all this.

'Yes. But don't worry if I can't. It'll only mean I can't get through. It won't mean anything's happened to the group, or to me.'

'I know. I won't worry. If anything happened it would be on the news. Perhaps I'll pray.'

The next time Georgia came in, she said, 'We're both clear about the time difference, aren't we?' They were, and had been for weeks. 'The first hint of danger,' she said, 'and I'll bottle out. I'm not going to waste having got to know you by taking any risks.'

'Good.'

'Your hair is wonderful, I'm so glad I did it.'

At twenty past eight everything was ready, and Georgia had her coat on. 'Passport, tickets, all in order,' she said. 'Health insurance. Checked and checked again. Money.' She inspected her bulging bag as she spoke. 'Lucky I don't have a cat.'

'Why? I could feed it. I would look after it.'

'Yes, you would. Oh dear, I hope I'm not going to cry.'

'Neither of us need. We shan't. I'll tidy up a bit here after you've gone.'

'Thank you. I'm just going to hug you in case the taxi's early.'

They hugged. The taxi was early. 'Better early than late,'

said Anne. The driver helped with the cases. Anne stood on the pavement and waved until she could see the taxi and its waving inmate no more. She went back into Georgia's house to wash up the cups. She did no serious tidying, not that much needed doing; she would be in the house every day for the vivarium, and could take her time.

It was a cold and drizzling November morning, at this hour not yet fully light, when Anne hurried down the street to her own house. John was in the kitchen.

'Did you remember I wouldn't be here?' Anne asked him.

'No, but I remembered when I didn't see you.'

'Have you had breakfast?'

'Yes, and I'm just going.' Off went John.

Anne sat down with a cup of tea. Then she texted Georgia, 'So sad to see you go.' Georgia, from the taxi, texted back immediately, 'Yes I am sad too.'

United by emotion, divided by steadily increasingly distance, each sat and thought about the other. Anne thought how different it was for Georgia, who had the journey to cope with, and then the interest and excitement of meeting her colleagues, some of whom she already knew, and then the long, dusty drive to the home of these remarkable creatures dear to her, the desert snails. She would miss Anne, Anne knew; but there would be much else to fill her mind and heart. Anne would have ordinary life. She would manage. But how flat ordinary life now seemed, without Georgia.

She picked up a couple of pieces of buttered bread left over from John's breakfast and pressed them together in a rough sandwich. With this and her tea she went into the sitting-room and sat down under the portrait, which had been hung in a good place on the wall, demoting a couple of other pictures. She looked at it. She felt quietly and intensely happy to have Georgia. She also felt happy that, out of nowhere, her own love had sprung into being. Perhaps that was the real miracle. Love was easier for Georgia. Georgia had led the way.

She heard Eric moving about, and automatically got up and went into the kitchen, finishing her bread and tea as she went. She began to arrange things for his breakfast, and smiled a welcome as he came in.

'Has the paper come?' he asked.

'Not yet.' This was a familiar opening. Eric sat down. 'What's this buttered bread doing here?' he asked, for such a platter on the table at this hour was not what he was used to.

'John's breakfast.'

There was a short silence from Eric, then a groan. 'I clean forgot,' he said.

'It doesn't matter.'

'No, I clean forgot. I was going to get up early and make breakfast for all three of us. I was going to greet you when you came back from Georgia's, all cold and hungry. I can't believe I clean forgot. I was going to do bacon butties, just as you used to like them, and the big teapot. I just can't believe I had the whole plan made, the bacon bought, and then I clean forgot every scrap of it.'

'Shall we say it's the thought that counts,' said Anne, who was actually feeling that the reality would have been rather cheering.

He saw through this mindless consolation. 'Shall I make them now? The butties?'

'I think the moment's passed.' She brought him toast.

Chewing, he said, 'I thought you would be a bit miz to say goodbye to Georgia. I wanted to cheer you up. You are going to miss her.'

'Yes, I am,' said Anne, and she turned away as her eyes stung with tears.

'You will have to make do with your old man for a couple of months.'

Anne was touched by this, and also by the word 'miz', which, like the bacon butties, came from their remote past. 'My old man's not so bad,' she said. 'Perhaps he can do the bacon butties for our lunch.'

Chapter 17

F our o'clock on a day in late November. Tally was walking
down the street in the direction of Anne and Eric's. She
did not stop at her own house to drop off her school bag,
nor did she need to tell Beale where she was going, for he
would know. A car drew up slowly beside her. The passenger
door opened and a hand shot out, grabbing Tally's wrist.

This was a good opportunity for the driver of the car, for
no one was to be seen on either of the damp, dark pavements,
except an old geezer on a stick, who was walking unsteadily
because the pavement was slippery, and who didn't count for
anything. It was the best opportunity yet. The man pulled,
Tally resisted. Tally screamed. 'Scream again and it'll be this
for you,' the man said, twisting her wrist. He could always
show her the knife, thought he, if she went on resisting. Tally
gasped with pain and fought silently for her wrist, but it
remained in the man's grip. At that moment Max Packington,
for he it was on the pavement, brought his stick down with
extraordinary force on the man's arm. There was a groan from
the man, but he was not yet deterred. Then Max dealt the
arm a second ferocious blow, and a third. The man was groaning
and swearing, three fingers broken. Tally was screaming again,
encouraged by the presence of Max, and Max was barking at
the top of his voice 'Help! Murder!' again and again.

Doors began to open at that end of the street. Juan and Maria Garcia's house was the nearest, and Juan was coming out of his front door, yelling in Spanish, while Maria stood in the lighted front window, watching steadily and dialling 999. Hugh Davis heard the commotion and burst out of his house and ran down the street, dialling 999 and taking note of the car's make and number. The man perceived it was all up, and let go of Tally's wrist. He slammed the passenger door shut and drove off with a scream of tyres, but not before he had hit out at Max Packington with the knife intended for Tally, and not before Max had fallen on his knees in the gutter. Maria Garcia, in her front window, the children beside her, imperturbably phoned 999 again, this time for an ambulance.

Beale took Tally in his arms. He was crying and shaking. 'Tally, are you all right?'

'I'm cool,' said Tally, 'but Mr Packington is dead.'

It was true. The blade of the man's knife had penetrated Max's aorta. The wound was fatal, and its outcome quick. Much of the bleeding was internal, but all the same there was quite a lot of blood soaking into Max's raincoat, and accumulating in the damp, leafy gutter where he lay.

The police and the ambulance arrived simultaneously, parking crookedly with lights flashing, making the street seem very narrow. Juan Garcia and Finola Hodgkins public-spiritedly drove their parked cars a few streets away to make more room. Almost everyone who was at home was now on his or her doorstep, or out in the street. Anne and Eric and John walked up from their end. It was getting darker. Everyone was quiet and kept a certain distance. The few street dwellers who knew what had happened and those to whom they had already imparted the story were in whispered demand. Max's body was neatly and discreetly picked up by the paramedics and taken away with bells and lights. After this, people felt more entitled to speak in normal voices. The police had found Max's mobile, and Isabel Packington was contacted. Anne realised that Mrs Gray had not appeared, and rang the doorbell of Number One. Mrs Gray answered and had to go through astonishment, dismay and, finally, grief. Harry and John had squeezed through to be near Tally, as the police questioned her. Then Beale, Harry and Tally were carried off to A and E in a police car to get attention for Tally's wrist. All this time Beale was desperately trying to reach Sally on her various phones, and finally succeeded, and the poor frantic woman headed straight for the hospital. The police began to tape off an area of the street as a crime scene. Mel Davis did not like the way Max's puddled blood glinted in the light of the the street lamps. It seemed disrespectful. She had planned to come later with a watering can to wash it away, but the crime scene development, which she had not foreseen, made this impossible. The blood belonged to the police now, as did the marks of the man's car tyres as he fled, and Max Packington's walking stick. A policeman stood on guard near the Garcias' front gate. Everyone was quiet, polite and friendly. There were few who did not long to help, but no help was needed.

The press arrived. Some street dwellers were interviewed, but many melted away into the anonymity of their houses. They all watched the TV news, however, and some found it difficult to recognise their street, not because it was distorted or misrepresented in the photographs, but because they had not seen the street on film before. Palmerston Street briefly became well known, and so did Max Packington, in a heroic mode he would have repudiated. When Cath arrived that evening to open Pam's, she realised that the notoriety would be good for business, which it was, as during the next week or two quite a few outside people wanted to have a look at the street, and ended their visit with a drink. Cath did not attempt to rope in Beale; she felt that would be bad taste in the circumstances.

Public interest died down, but there were recurrences. One was almost immediate, when the man with the horrible face, for he it was, was tracked down and arrested. Three recent crimes of abduction, sexual assault and murder of little girls of which he was the perpetrator were thereby solved. The horrible face filled television screens for a day or two, and it revived later, when the man was sentenced to life in such a way that it meant life. A minor recurrence was Max's funeral, delayed for three weeks by the inquest. It earned a mention on the news, but by that point many watchers had forgotten why he was important.

~

John came to find Anne as she sat at her patchwork. She sat at a different angle when, as now, she was busy with it on the sewing machine. Because of the rhythmic hum she had not heard John's approach. She stopped the treadle at once and turned and looked at him over her glasses. She smiled warmly. 'Well, darling,' she said.

'Granny.'

'Yes?'

'Do I have to go to Canada?'

'Do you have to go to Canada?'

'Yes.'

Anne turned round completely and gave him all her attention. She did not know what to say. She was astonished by the question. 'I thought,' she began, but did not attempt to finish the sentence. What was the sense in telling John what she had thought? So she was silent.

John was silent as well, and his mouth worked with suppressed tears and the lump in his throat. Should Anne notice, she wondered, or was it better not? After a little while she said, 'Why?'

John spoke huskily. 'I think Tally might like . . . I think Tally might want . . .'

Anne stood up and put her arms round him. She held him tight and stroked his head and he cried, his tears soaking into her cardigan. Then she said, 'Yes. Of course Tally might like and of course Tally would want. But there are two more weeks before you're supposed to be leaving. And then you'll be back three weeks after that. Tally will miss you, of course she will. But you will be back.'

John dealt as best he could with crying. When he could speak, he said with a wail in his voice that made him sound much younger, 'But I don't want to go at all!'

Anne could not help feeling pleased that the grandson she had assumed all autumn was pining for his mother was, in fact, attached to the home and the life she and Eric offered him. She did not have to wonder any more about what a proper grandmother would do. She *was* a proper grandmother. Whatever she did and said would be what a proper grandmother would do and say. This was a huge relief and made her very happy both for herself and for John. She stood gently stroking his head. At the same time she felt concerned for Sara. How would Sara take John's reluctance to join his family? Anne hoped she need never know. John's distress would probably blow over. Anne was also grappling with an unworthy question about whether if the worst came to the worst the air fare would be refunded. She rather thought it would not.

'I've got an idea,' said Anne, when John's sobs had quietened. 'Will you come with me to the vivarium? And why don't you ring Tally and see if she would like to come? Neither of you have seen it yet.'

Tally was beginning to be out and about again, but she had not yet been round to John's. He was not sure why not. He did not want what had happened with the man with the horrible face and with Mr Packington to make a difference. Tally's hand was still strapped up, so you could not feel that things were really back to normal.

John dialled her number and she answered at once. She did want to go to the vivarium, and she did want to come to tea afterwards. She waited outside Georgia's house for Anne and John.

'If you have to go to Canada,' Tally said to John, 'I'll come in and feed the pigeons.'

'Good,' said John. 'Does Anne know?'

'Not yet but she won't mind.'

'No.'

'And I'll visit Benn's grave at the same time.'

'Cool.'

John and Tally looked for snails among the greenery in the vivarium while Anne adjusted the water and the food. 'You'll probably see some,' said Anne. 'It's a damp day and not cold. That's their weather.'

'Look,' said John. A big tabby snail was hurrying up the clear plastic wall of the vivarium. John and Tally watched with fascination. 'You can see the muscles of its underside moving,' said Tally.

'Yes. I don't suppose they are muscles, exactly.'

'What are they?'

'We can ask Georgia.'

'But she's away.'

'She'll be back.' There was a silence while they watched the snail.

'Why do people think snails are slow? This one's whizzing,' said Tally.

'Yes. Look, it's lifting up the tip of its tail as it whizzes.'

'That's to whizz better.'

'Yes.'

John felt that everything was all right again.

~

The next time Anne was alone with Eric they had this conversation.

'John's saying he doesn't want to go to Canada for Christmas.'

'He doesn't want to go to Canada for Christmas?'

'Yes.'

'Well,' said Eric, thinking of his daughter, 'he has to go.' There was a silence while they pondered. 'He's upset by what happened to Tally, probably. There's time for that to wear off.'

'We've got a date for Max's funeral. It's the day before John leaves. So he won't have to be away for that.'

'Good. He wouldn't want to miss that. The whole street will be there.'

'Except Georgia.'

'Except Georgia. Have you heard from her, I mean in the last few days?'

'Yes. Confirmation that the trip is absolutely safe. The group is in a friendly village and there are no hostilities anywhere near, and there are lots of snails.'

'Good. You must have told her about what happened.'

'Yes. She was sorry for Tally and sad about Max and furious with the man.'

'Like us all,' said Eric. Then, 'Was this on email?' he enquired, hoping the phone bill was not soaring.

'Yes,' said Anne, who knew exactly why the question was asked, but was not going to let it annoy her.

'John will have to go to Canada,' said Eric, thoughtfully. 'It's only for three weeks. I'll have a word with him.'

'You are a good grandfather,' Anne said, knowing she had used the same words before.

'It's easier to be a good grandfather than a good husband,' said Eric. 'But I am trying.'

~

Sweltering in her hat and sunglasses, Georgia was deeply shocked by the news. She re-read Anne's email many times. She answered it, conveying much more of how it had made her feel than Anne had seen fit to pass on to Eric. She told Anne how she shuddered and felt faint whenever she thought of the fate Tally had escaped, and how she could not get this out of her mind. She said it had made her sick in the night, and she asked for her love to be given to the Paces. She thought more vividly than before of the children who do not escape, and the thought chilled her blood.

Brenda at the beginning of autumn, Max at the end. Max's death did not make Georgia ask 'What is a life?' as Brenda's had, because she scarcely knew him. She didn't find herself hanging that huge question mark over all deaths, only close ones. But she thought about him, so far as acquaintance allowed, and retained a strong sense of him, courteous and white-haired, for several days. She thanked him from the bottom of her heart for what it seemed he had done for Tally. There would be no shortage of obituaries this time, she thought, and he would have a big, possibly a resplendent, funeral. He would be honoured in a way which Brenda, also deserving, had not been. It occurred to Georgia that two houses in the street would be For Sale when she got home, not just one, as she had expected. Eventually there would be new neighbours. Georgia was enjoying her field trip but looking forward to getting home.

~

'Now I've nearly been murdered,' said Tally to her parents, 'I don't see how you can stop me having a cat.'

Beale and Sally were nonplussed by this statement. They also saw the force of it.

'But what about me and Harry both being allergic?' said Sally. 'How are we going to get round that?'

'Harry's not that allergic,' said Tally. 'He was often in John's attic with Benn.'

'Don't pretend you'd have noticed if Harry had started sneezing and sniffing,' said Beale.

'Anyway,' said Sally, 'the cat might have been asleep. It's when its mouth parts get going that the organisms that make us allergic get into the air.'

'All right,' said Tally. 'The kitten will have to belong to John and me and will have to live at John's.'

'You can't land another cat on Anne and Eric,' said Sally.

'Yes, I can, I've asked them.'

'Asked them?'

'Yes. And the kitten can move in when John gets back from Canada. This is a secret, by the way. I want it to be a surprise for John.'

'Where's this kitten coming from?'

'Number Nineteen. Kittens have been born at Number Nineteen. Anne told me. Mrs Kane's cat, that's the scaredy black one with a collar the other side of the street, has had kittens and the Kanes will be looking for homes. The kittens will be ready to leave their mum when John gets back.'

'Good Lord, Tally,' said Beale, 'you've got it all worked out.'

'I'd better go down and have a word with poor Anne,' said Sally to Beale.

'Yes,' said Beale. 'We aren't the only ones who can't refuse you anything, it seems.'

'No, Dad, Anne was keen. I think she was keen.'

'Have you seen these kittens?'

'Yes. There are six. They are absolutely tiny now with their eyes shut. But they can miaow.'

Bernardine Bishop on Writing

There is a fifty-year gap between my first two novels, published precociously in my early twenties, and my third, *Unexpected Lessons in Love*. In between I married, had my children, divorced, trained as a teacher, retrained as a psychotherapist, lost my parents, lost my sister, welcomed my sons' partners into our family, had grandchildren, married again and got cancer. Never once, during those fifty years, did it occur to me that I might write fiction again.

The day after I was told that my cancer had gone, I sat down and began this book. It was as if I had taken my life back and it was up to me to do something different with it. I had not known until then that I was longing to write, but even after fifty years I recognised the feeling.

After the first chapter, I fell in love with what I was writing. I remember thinking 'this is easy'; I remember the excitement, the energy that seemed to have been waiting there for me to tap into. I remember the delight at being in control of my own story again. During my treatment for cancer, the endless hospital appointments, the chemo and radiotherapy sessions, the agony of waiting for results, of sitting in front of doctors who knew more than I did about my future, I ceded authority to others. Now at my desk, I took it back. Cancer was one journey; my book would be another.

And once I had finished *Unexpected Lessons in Love* I could not stop. Since childhood, words and stories have been my natural habitat. I would not describe my need to write as a compulsion exactly, but I am conscious of enjoying it more than anything else I have done, of feeling entirely confident in what I was doing. I began my next book almost straight away. If *Unexpected Lessons* draws on my preoccupation with cancer and my longing for recovery, on the love I feel for my sons, and on my experiences of mothering, then *Hidden Knowledge* draws on my experiences as a therapist. A darker novel, it explores the things people do not know about themselves, the things they cannot face.

And after *Hidden Knowledge*, I went straight on to *The Street*. It is my final novel, because when I finished it I thought: this is it. I have shot my bolt. And I was right because the oncologist was wrong: the cancer has returned. It seems that it never went away. I wish tremendously strongly that I could write another book, but I know I have no more stories in me; I am too handicapped by illness. It may also be that I have told the stories I have to tell because *The Street* – a story of friendship, of longing, of people coming together – ends with the good death of an old man. As I wrote the last words and shut down the computer, I thought: this is enough. I have finished.

Bernardine Bishop – A Biography

Bernardine Bishop was born in London in 1939, just two months before the outbreak of the Second World War. The great-granddaughter of the poet Alice Meynell, Bernardine, along with her elder sister Gabriel, spent her earliest years with her grandmother, Madeleine, at the home Alice and Wilfred Meynell created for their family and its descendants at Greatham in West Sussex. Greatham remains a place of great importance to Bernardine and her family.

Bernardine Bishop's parents, Bernard and Barbara Wall, among the leading Catholic intellectuals of their day, were in Rome when war broke out, remaining there until 1940. Her mother, under her maiden name of Barbara Lucas, went on to write eight novels and also worked as a journalist for the *Observer* and the *Spectator* and as a translator. Her father was a distinguished historian of the Catholic Church and worked for British Intelligence during the war.

On returning to England, Barbara Wall became a land girl on a farm in Oxfordshire and took her daughters to live with her there. The sudden wrench away from Greatham and her beloved grandmother caused Bernardine great unhappiness. Returning to London after the war, Bernardine was educated at various Catholic schools, eventually gaining a place to read English Literature at Newnham College, Cambridge. This was the era when dons like F. R. Leavis and C. S. Lewis held sway in the lecture theatres and seminar rooms. Among Bernardine's contemporaries were David Frost and Peter Cook, and her lifelong friend, the novelist Margaret Drabble.

In 1960, on leaving Cambridge, Bernardine Bishop was co-opted as the youngest witness in the *Lady Chatterley* trial. She went on to write two early novels, worked as a reviewer and journalist and in 1961 married the pianist Stephen Bishop (now Stephen Kovacevich), who had come to London to study under Dame Myra Hess. Their elder son, Matt, was born in 1962; their younger, Francis, in 1964. By 1965 Bernardine and Stephen Bishop had separated and their marriage was eventually annulled.

To support herself and her young sons, Bernardine Bishop turned to teaching, eventually becoming Head of English at a London comprehensive school. She then went on to have a distinguished career as a psychotherapist, training at the London Centre for Psychotherapy and also working as a tutor and supervisor. She co-wrote a number of books on psychotherapy and contributed to many academic and professional journals. Cancer forced her retirement in 2010 and she returned to her first love, fiction. Of the three novels she wrote during this period, the first, *Unexpected Lessons in Love*, was published in January 2013. *Hidden Knowledge* is the second and it was followed by *The Street*. Until her death in July 2013, Bernardine Bishop lived in London with her husband, Bill Chambers, whom she married in 1981.

Hidden Knowledge

an extract from Bernardine Bishop's previous book,
available from Sceptre

Bernardine Bishop

Chapter 1

It was the first anniversary of Betty Winterborne's husband's death. She sat down with a cup of coffee and looked out of the window. It was exactly the same view as she had looked at a year ago, the trees coming into leaf; the pigeons cheerfully flapping among the twigs; the houses opposite with the sun on them. This was the chair on which she had habitually sat after Jack's bed had been brought downstairs. She had sat here to chat with him, then to read to him, and then, in the final weeks, just to sit.

She was slightly irked that she must make a thing of the anniversary, and she didn't know what special thoughts or feelings to have. Close friends would remember to telephone; her daughter would probably feel she must mark the day somehow. But what was special about it? Now, however, sitting in the chair and looking out of the window, Betty felt she was getting an inkling. The branches of the tree were at exactly the same point, with regard to bud, leaf and pigeons, as they had been at the moment when she had heard Jack's first respiratory pause. 'Life must go on,' people had said to her a year ago. Why must it? What if it doesn't? But now she saw that it had. There was, after all, something to be said for an anniversary. Spring had come again. She was pleased to see it.

There was another less public anniversary, for it was at this time of year – not the day, exactly, but the season, and the general stage of the pigeons and the leaves – that, two years ago, Jack had been diagnosed. Betty and Jack had endured a year of the snakes and ladders that cancers and hospitals impose. Then, one year ago to the day, they had lost.

Betty was lonely. Loneliness must be differentiated from missing Jack. She did miss Jack. But the loneliness that gnawed her away was not the same as the missing of Jack, though it was easy to confuse the two, and, she felt, plenty of people might not bother to draw the distinction. Certainly, her friends did not do so, in their warm care of her widowhood. Only she knew that all her life, the fear of loneliness had been what moved her into action. She had married young, as she had intended to, for marriage and children were the insurance against loneliness. Not for her the hope that if she waited long enough she would find the unequivocal love another part of her longed to experience. She was a romantic, but she could not boldly live as a romantic, as some of her friends had continued to do into their late twenties, or, with hope dwindling, further. Jack was a good bet. He was tall and good-looking, had a First in Law, everyone liked him, and he was in love with her. Jack would do, and no one around her detected that what looked like romance was raw practicality. Jack had never known.

They had been happy. Jack had worked hard and was successful. Betty, who had read Modern Languages, pursued a more desultory career, featuring evening classes, tutoring and translations. She had not minded. She had liked being a help to Jack. She had taken pleasure in managing the social life his work generated. She had enjoyed keeping house. They had two children.

And all the time, for forty years, Betty had been one of a couple. The wolf of loneliness had not only been kept from the regularly painted front door of the North London Victorian terraced house in which Betty and Jack lived; the wolf had been forgotten. The fear of the wolf had been forgotten. The wolf had died, or turned into a fairy-tale, or a lapdog. Other frightening beasts had called, and one had ravaged her. But she had not known loneliness, or the terror of it. She had heard, without hearing, Jack's key in the lock at about seven every evening. Every day, she had planned, without planning, supper for two. She was aware, without rejoicing, of his presence in bed beside her. If there was time to watch a television programme, she would not watch it alone. If he was out, he was going to come home. If he was in, and both were working, one of them would soon, without noticing a motivation, go and find the other.

'I hate dying,' Jack had said. 'But I'm lucky, dying first.'

If Betty had died first, she thought, Jack would have missed her. He would have missed her, perhaps, more than she missed him. But it would have been different for him, because he did not have the predisposition to innate loneliness that for forty years had been secreting itself, unfelt but unaltered, deep inside her. He would have been lonely, but, once the worst of the missing had passed, he would not have been crippled by loneliness itself. And then, she thought, like many widowers, he would quite likely have replaced her.

For her, replacement would be difficult, even if any man were to look at a woman of sixty. Any antidote to loneliness depended on long-standing familiarity, depended as much on not having to have conversations as on being easily able to, as much on the known footsteps on the floor above as on being in the same room. This was why Betty's social life in the last year had not helped as much as friends had hoped it might.

However, another feeling had crept in gradually of late. This was a sense that her loneliness could, possibly, be met as a challenge, rather than suppressed as a malady. This was a new idea. She had never, in her quite long life, allowed herself to suffer her loneliness. She had evaded it. Perhaps to endure its darkness and coldness, instead of automatically switching on lights and turning up heating, was a necessary step for her towards maturity. She liked this thought. She did not want to die with her bogeys unfaced. Her grandfather had been killed on the Somme; her father had survived the D Day landings and never said a word about it. There was a toughness in Betty that she had never used. She had always been afraid it wasn't there. She hoped to be able to use it now, and she prayed it would be up to the job.

The telephone rang. It was Betty's daughter, Julia.

'Just remembering what day it is, Mum,' said Julia.

'Thank you.'

'How are you?'

'I'm fine.'

'What are you just doing? I've only got a moment, I'm between patients.'

'Having a cup of coffee. Being glad spring has come again.'

'Good. Are you doing anything this evening? I'll come over. With a bunch of flowers.'

'That's lovely. At about eight? We'll eat.' The problem of evening that day was solved, and as congenially as could be.

Betty thought about Julia. She was uneasy about Julia not being married, at thirty-eight. She used the word 'married' in her own mind, but if talking to a friend she would have said 'settled', to avoid seeming old-fashioned. Julia had been in two long relationships, but neither had ended in settledness. Conceivably, she had not wanted them to. Now past her first bloom, she was alone and childless. She threw herself into her work and was cheerful, and Betty saw no signs that her own loneliness was hereditary. But what a shame. That was the trouble these days. The women's movement seemed to have left the world even more a man's world than it was already. Betty thought that if she were young now she would not stand a chance of seeing how to cope. She admired Julia her hardihood.

~

'We must have a proper talk, tonight,' said Hereward Tree. He was speaking Italian. He looked steadily, his eyes intent and yearning, at Carina, beautiful, lively, and over thirty years his junior. She did not answer, but sat down beside him and took his hand.

He went on, 'Obviously I hope I will come through the operation alive and well. But it is a big operation, and I may not. You do realise that, don't you, darling?'

'I have looked it up on the internet. Usually people are all right.'

'Usually people may not have smoked quite as much as me.'

'No. But you are thin. That is important as well.' Carina shifted a little to be closer to him, and he smelt her scent. Whether he lived or whether he died, he thought, he had this moment.

'I love you,' said Hereward. It was a statement in which his whole life and self, at that stage of his life and self, were expressed. He hoped she realised she did not need to answer with a trite reciprocation. She said nothing, and looked at him tenderly. One of the wonderful things about her was that she understood when to let an utterance from his soul resonate and remain.

After a moment's pause he went on. 'Tomorrow. Don't come and see me tomorrow. I shall be a mass of tubes and will not know whether you are there or not. Wait for Romola to tell you when to come.'

'I am afraid of Romola.'

'That doesn't matter. I know you are. In the next few days she will telephone and tell you when to come to the hospital. If all goes well I shall be home in a couple of weeks. We have a full time carer moving in. That is all arranged. You will not have to do anything for me. You will just sometimes let me look at you.'

'I will be afraid of the carer.'

'You'll get used to her.'

'I will want to do things to help.'

'OK, but you won't have to.'

'I shall cook meals.'

'OK, do that. Now, that is how it will probably be. But, on the other hand, I may die. If I do, Romola will inform you. I'm sorry about that.'

'But you will not die.'

'I hope not. In my will, I have left you all my money and this house, with everything in it. I have only left Romola the literary stuff. But now I want to give you a piece of very serious advice. If I die, I think you should go home to Genoa. You will have money, once the – ' Hereward did not know the Italian for the word probate, so said 'will', again – 'once the will is through. Later you will have a lot of money from the sale of this house and the quite valuable things in it. Romola must organise the sale for you, and the money will be all yours.'

'I don't want to think about what if you die,' said Carina, who had, actually, been rather taken with the scenario.

'So now make love with me. Make love until morning. We haven't done that for a long time.'

'Yes, we will. But we will have supper first. Don't forget you aren't allowed to eat or drink after midnight. Anyway I am starving. So I will cook something now.'

Hereward was not hungry. He reluctantly let go of her hand and watched her hurry in the direction of the kitchen. Her back view was purposeful, and he smiled. Indeed he chuckled. After a minute he stood up, breathing heavily, leaning on a stick, and followed her. He could watch her cook. He did not want to miss a moment.

~

Roger Tree ran through the spring rain and encroaching dusk. His raincoat, heavy anyway, and with things in its pockets thumping his thighs, was now also wet. He arrived at his sister's front door and rang the bell.

Romola Tree had sat down to her marking. It used always to be a pile of exercise books, but now, of course, like everything else, it was typewritten and submitted in folders, which she found more difficult to transport than the exercise books had been. Nowadays she usually drove to and from the school where she worked. It was a short distance, and it would have done very well for the daily walk we are all advised to take, and she regretted forfeiting it. But, hardworked and with an Ofsted looming, she could not take the time to think about her health. At fifty-five, she was at the height of her responsibilities, head both of her department and of a house. On her desk, as well as the pile of folders, were a cup of tea and a plate heavy with crispbread and cheese. She marked, sipped and nibbled; but she was not contented with her lot.

When the weekend came, she would sit at the same desk, with no school folders and no plate. And she would get on with her novel.

It was her fourth novel, and its three predecessors had been turned down. She had an agent, but the agent was unenthusiastic, and the publishers, adamant. She persisted because it was what she enjoyed doing. She always had hopes, of course, as she did this time; and occasionally, when sleepless, made up her speech for the Booker Prize award night. Her first novel had been a fictionalised account of Wordsworth's relationship with Annette Vallon. The second had done much the same for Keats and Fanny Brawne. The next one was called *Withering Depths*, and had been a mistake, though still, at least in her own view, not without its subtleties. Now she was blissfully engaged on an ending for Mrs Gaskell's *Wives and Daughters*.

Because of her lack of success, she did not broadcast her novel-writing. But people who got to know her at all could not avoid realising it was her hobby and passion. Word went round. The headmistress had recently ribbed her about it. 'Like brother, like sister, eh?' she had said. Romola had not liked this. It was patronising. Her novels were not derivative of Hereward's. When Hereward and Romola were children, Romola, a year the younger, had been as inventive as Hereward. She had been as creative, and more literary. A mad wife had crept into their games, before Hereward had even heard of *Jane Eyre*. Romola's voice-overs belonged to the written word of Victorian novels, while Hereward's were colloquial, and, to Romola's mind, banal. It was Romola who wrote up in a succession of exercise books – she still had them – the stories that evolved from the antics of the job lot of dolls and toy animals laid out on the attic floor. Romola loved the game more than Hereward did. Sometimes she would say, 'Let's go upstairs for Hanulaland,' and he, for a minute, would look as if he would as soon be doing something else. But he had to come. He knew it was not a game you could play alone, and he knew you became absorbed, as in nothing else.

It was entirely their own. When Roger became able to climb the ladder to the attic, and his little face, smiling and triumphant, appeared suddenly one afternoon at floor level, Hereward and Romola stared at it with horror. 'You aren't allowed,' cried Romola, and at the same time, from Hereward, 'What are you doing here?'

A gentler version of that expression was on Romola's face now, when she saw who was on the doorstep, cowering from the rain. 'Roger!' she exclaimed.

'Can I come in?'

'Yes, come in. But I've got a pile of marking to do before tomorrow.' She helped him hang his raincoat, and took him into the sitting-room, where, indeed, her marking was manifest. 'I suppose I know why you've come,' she said.

Roger looked astonished, then nervous. 'How could you know?'

'Hereward. Going into hospital tomorrow for his operation. You might be upset. But obviously that's got nothing to do with it.'

'Tomorrow? Is it? I had forgotten. I knew it was coming up, of course. Oh, dear – poor him. Triple heart bypass, isn't it?'

'Yes.' Romola didn't like to hear the operation called by its name, and disliked Roger for glibly so calling it, as if to compensate, by cheap medical lingo, for the fact that it had gone from his mind. For Romola, Hereward's state of health was a constant preoccupation. To hear the surgical procedure mentioned at this point jolted her into fresh spasms of anxiety. 'I'm sure he'll be all right,' she said, reassuring herself, as Roger did not require reassurance. 'Loads of people have them these days. The words make them sound worse than they are.' From having looked at a video of the operation on the internet, she knew this was not true.

'Well, why are you here, then?' she asked. She had still not offered him a drink. If he had a drink, she would probably have one, then she would have another, and then she would have lost her appetite for marking. Perhaps a cup of tea, but she could not be bothered.

'I wondered whether you could put me up.'

'Put you up? Why? Whatever's happened?'

'I can't explain. I suppose I should say that I don't want to explain. I'm sorry.'

'For heaven's sake! Have you lost your faith? Have you punched a parishioner? Have you run off with a parishioner's wife? Have you embezzled the collection boxes?'

But Roger was silent, staring at the floor. How could he smile at these sallies? He was unhappier than he had ever been in his life. Meanwhile his shoes were soaked, leaving traces on Romola's carpet, and he badly wanted a drink. 'None of the above,' he answered in a croaky voice.

'Tea, coffee or a drink?' said Romola, disconcerted to hear signs of tears. 'Have you had anything to eat?'

'Nothing to eat, thanks.'

She poured him a scotch, abstaining, so far, herself. She still hoped that the contours of her planned evening could be restored, but now she was becoming curious about Roger and what had brought him to her door. "You might as well tell me,' she said.

'OK.' He had drunk his scotch in two swallows, and his face seemed to Romola to be a better colour already. 'Can I have another?'

She responded by putting the bottle on a table at his elbow. He refilled his glass.

'I'm on bail,' he said. 'A young person I knew in my last parish has been to the police. He has said I sexually abused him. This is going back more than ten years. The police came, I was arrested, and suspended immediately from priestly duties.

I can't stay in the presbytery. I could have, physically, but gossip was starting already. I have to disappear from the parish. I don't know where to go. I can't possibly stay in my presbytery. The bishop wasn't much help, though I know him, we were curates together years ago. This is absolutely dreadful. And all in a day, out of a clear blue sky.'

'And why is the young man making this accusation against you?'

Roger was silent. Then, for the first time that evening, he looked Romola in the eye. 'Because it's true,' he said.

There was a longer silence, a stunned one for Romola. She fetched another glass and poured herself a scotch. 'Not such a clear blue sky, then,' she said. Then she asked, 'Did you tell the police it was true?'

'Yes.'

Romola's face relaxed a little from its rictus of extreme censure. That admission must have taken some courage.

Roger went on, 'I couldn't make him – Tony is his name – feel disbelieved. It happened, and he is telling the truth. But why he has taken it into his head to come out with it ten – more like fifteen – years later, of course I have no idea. We have corresponded about it in the past. I thought it was at rest.'

'At rest,' said Romola. 'Is that what the cover-ups are called? At rest!'

Hereward and Romola had never tried to understand Roger's conversion to the Catholic Church, nor his entering the priesthood. But they had treated these things with the greatest respect, joking about them, if at all, only with each other. Both of them had turned up for his baptism and for his ordination. Their mother had come with them, but their father was not persuadable. 'Did he but know it, he's only doing this to spite Dad,' whispered Romola to Hereward. 'Shhh,' said Hereward, who was liking the ceremonial. Hereward's sympathies were wider than Romola's, to her chagrin. She thought this was because he had a happier life.

'Hereward will have to know,' said Romola.

'I know. Everyone will have to know.'

'You poor thing.'

'I thought, being a novelist, Hereward might think something like "nihil humanum a me alienum puto".'

'Nonsense. It would be "alienum" to anyone except another paedophile.'

The word 'paedophile' stabbed Roger, rather as the phrase 'triple heart bypass' had Romola. But he bowed his head. What could he say? After a minute he repeated his earlier plea. 'Look, I'm awfully sorry, but can I stay with you? Probably not for very long.'

'Not for very long?' What he meant began to dawn on her. 'You're saying?'

'Yes. It'll be prison. Of course.'

～

Romola got up at five, hung over, to finish her marking. From the spare bedroom Roger heard her moving about quietly, probably trying not to disturb him. He had not slept, and so needed no such consideration. But he was grateful for it, and grateful that his sister had taken him in. He went over in his mind what he had to do – there was to be a committal, this morning, and various subsequent dates with police and probation, before his hearing came up.

He was intensely miserable. Around midnight he had closed the spare room door behind him, and his mind went back a couple of years, to the last time he had been in this room, in which his mother had lain dying, and had died. He knelt in prayer, leaning on a chair. He was not particularly tipsy, in spite of the whisky. Grief and fear seemed to have consumed the alcohol before his system had been able to. At this point he did not pray for forgiveness or for Tony; he had done that twelve years before. Now he prayed for courage. Then he did not pray for anything, but just prayed.

Then he took off a few clothes. His shoes and socks, and the bottoms of his trousers, were still soaking wet, so he arranged them on the radiator, which was tepid now, but perhaps would be warm by morning. He crept under the duvet. Hopkins's words, 'Creep, wretch, under a comfort, serves in a whirlwind', came into his mind. But in his case there was no comfort, however small, however derisory, to creep under.

If he could put his situation out of his mind, just for the time being, he would be able to sleep, and that would help him face tomorrow. But he could not put it out of his mind, for it was in his body. Even without specific thoughts, he was beset by the shivers and palpitations of fear, the dry mouth and the churning guts; and he was gripped by the heaviness and pressure of grief, an iron case drawn tight around his chest.

Lying as still as he could, sometimes too hot and sometimes too cold, he tried to think. In a fundamental way, his state was no different from what it had been twenty-four hours ago, when he had gone to bed thinking about the money for the church roof, whether he could stir his parishioners into concern over climate change, and, indeed, whether the diocese would approve solar panels, as the roof had to be done anyway. What luxurious worries these seemed now. That self was gone. It was gone for ever. There was this new self now, crying and sighing, throwing the duvet off and on again.

But fundamentally, there was no difference between yesterday evening and this. Yesterday, as much as today, he was the man who had committed the crimes he was accused of. Fundamentally, his crimes, and the harm he had done by them, were what mattered. The fact that he was now unmasked was trivial by comparison. This he told himself. But what grieved and terrified him in an immediate and physical sense was the fact that he had been found out.

He could feel with his conscience, though not with his body, that the facts that he would cease to be a priest in good standing, and that he would be sent to prison, were relatively trivial. He would suffer. That was just. He had not, after all, been a priest in good standing twenty-four hours ago. It was merely that people thought he was. But not everything that belonged to his good standing was trivial. He had been trusted by his parishioners, in his present parish, in the one before, and in the one before that. He had betrayed them. Twenty-four hours ago, he was already someone who had betrayed them. But twenty-four hours ago they did not know it. Now they did. He groaned in an agony that was far from trivial when he thought of Nora and Seamus, Xavier, Bernadette, Karol, Mbeke, Mrs Rafferty, and, oh, so many others, when they heard the news. Of course he would lose their love and respect, and he had loved their love and respect; but that belonged to the realm of triviality, and that loss to justice. What mattered was that they might lose faith in what he had tried to stand for, the hopes and aspirations whither he had tried to lead. And, of course, they would be without a parish priest, when priests are in short supply.

He got up and knelt at the chair again, to pray for his parishioners. If only it could be he that was the only one to suffer. But it could not be so. Suddenly he thought of, and prayed for, the mothers of the babies he had baptised. What would their feelings be? Let them keep faith with the Sacrament, he prayed, if not with its minister. He went back to bed, noticing that he reeked of sweat. In this next stage of the night he had another thought. Some of his parishioners would forgive him. It would take time. They would struggle inwardly; they would talk together; Damian or Maria might call a parish meeting. Many different views would be expressed. Many would pray for him. Some would say we are all human. Some would be too angry to say that, some too astounded to say anything. The bishop, Pip Jenkins, an old friend of Roger's, would have to make a formal visitation to the parish. Thinking of them forgiving him, perhaps lighting a candle for him, Roger sobbed.

Now it occurred to him for the first time that he could write a letter. Maria would see that it was read out at all the Masses one weekend. He would send it care of Maria. Sentences for the letter started to shape in his mind, and the letter began to serve as some sort of comfort in a whirlwind, for his wretched self to creep under.

The best books live on in your head long after they are finished. As you read, you are turning the pages faster and faster to find out what happens next, only to feel bereft when you reach the end.

If that is how you feel now, you might like to join us at www.hodder.co.uk, or follow us on Twitter @hodderbooks, and be part of our community of people who love the very best of books and reading.

Whether you want to find out more about this book, or a particular author, watch trailers and interviews, have the chance to win early limited editions, or simply browse our expert readers' selection of the very best books, we think you'll find what you're looking for.

And if you don't, that's the place to tell us what's missing.

We love what we do, and we'd love you to be part of it.

www.hodder.co.uk

@hodderbooks

HodderBooks

HodderBooks